LaToya-Monique

Copyright 2017

Story By: LaToya-Monique Warren

Editing and Digital Formatting By: Author Everlazt

Cover Art and graphics By: Author Everlazt

Published By: EverDomo LLC

To nena,
Thank you for supporting me.
please enjoy!
Thank you for starting a new journey with me
Blessings!

About The Author

LaToya-Monique was born and raised in Queens, N. Y. where she found her love for writing at the tender age of eleven. LaToya-Monique penned her first poem called 'Wishing Well', entered it into a poetry contest and won. That inspired LaToya-Monique to take the long journey to becoming a published author.

LaToya-Monique love for writing became a career when she penned numerous articles, interviews, and became Editor and Chief of 24sevennights Magazine. Seeing the need to reach a broader audience LaToya-Monique birthed her own LM Movement and YouTube talk show 'Let's Talk About It with LaToya-Monique'.

LaToya-Monique dedicates her time and energy into the uplifting of the ordinary/extraordinary individual who would like their voice heard. Giving people a voice on her talk show was a dream come true and creating events for the new up and coming people of talent is her mission. She is building people in the community, as she continues to build on herself. LaToya-Monique hopes to continue to grow in this industry and touch as many lives as she can by using her writing, talk show, and movement as powerful tools.

<u>Dedication Page</u>

This book would not have been birthed if it wasn't for a
company firing me with no good cause. That experience allowed me to
wake up in knowing that my purpose was bigger than working a nine to
five. I was convinced that I was created for so much more. In that time
of my life I kept the burning flame of resiliency, blocked the world out
and started to create the characters in my mind. I wanted to create a
book that made people think and feel. I wanted to allow people
permission that it's ok to go into their fantasy part of their minds and
make magic happen. I found out that it was okay to express your
sexuality and still be a lady at the end of the day. Cabin Love/Letters Of
Fate opens up Pandora's box that engage what is right and what wrong
in the daily decision making in lives.

I want to first thank God for making all things possible. I had to
learn that nothing in this world happens without the hand of God
allowing you grace and mercy. Jesus is real in my life.

Thank you to each of my pre-editor readers, that read Cabin
Love/Letters of Fate, unedited, raw copy. Each of them gave me the
perception that my book was a best seller. Jasmine Parris, Yamese
Williams, Chevonne Campbell, Katiya Lyons Kareem Collins,Charlene
B Williams, Robert Warren Jr. Cierra Warren, Jesimiel Arrington,
Gloria Parris and Patricia Bello.

I want to thank my three daughters for putting up with my
dreams when there was no money, no fame, no justice, only constant

struggle and yet they still believed in me because they seen a fire in me that was burning even when I couldn't smell the smoke.

A special thanks to my good friend and business partner, Author Everlazt. Over a 2-decade friendship that God allowed to manifest to this. I want to thank him for putting the fire behind me and believing in me. He took all he had inside him and transferred that energy into me to allow me to believe that this book could be birthed. His friendship is priceless to me.

I thank my good, good girlfriend Sheila Phillips for holding me and my daughters down while we were fighting on of the biggest fights in our lives. With all that I have, I want to sincerely recreate the Golden Girls theme song, and say "thank you for being a friend" ....I love you so much. Sheila and her two daughters Skylar and Sharia was our bridge over troubled waters.

Who would I be if I didn't thank my parents in heaven. Martha P Mayes, and Robert Lee Warren. I thank them for giving me a mirror of what being kind to people really means. I know that each of them, did the best they could in loving my sister, brother and I. May each of their souls Rest in Peace. Mommy, I did it!

Last and never least I truly dedicate this book to every woman that has ever endured pain and suffering in a relationship with someone who didn't appreciate the value she put into it. My wish for you is that you find your Wolfe.

Cabin Love
The Letters Of Fate

Written by:

LaToya-Monique

LACY

The Cabin

My red suitcase and matching overnight bag sat at my front door, I did another walk around of the house to make sure that no candles were lit accidently and that the oven along with all lights were cut off in the house. Our house smelled of fresh strawberries from the homemade candles that our neighbor Mrs. Krauss gives us every spring. It was a hobby she picked up after retiring as a social worker for the state. I left one small light in the living room on so the house didn't look disserted over the weekend.

My fiancé Bradley took my daughter ShyAnn to his mother's house for the weekend. Bradley's sister is getting married early summer and this was her engagement party. I couldn't make it this weekend I had something that I had to do way more important so that I can get my life back together.

I am a freelance photographer and started taking pictures when I was a little girl. My dad brought my first expensive camera when I was fourteen. I am still amazed the love that I have for photos, catching moments in my photos that people can never live again unless they look back at a picture.

With the passion within me I started my own studio at home and pick up clients from the word of mouth. I make double Bradley's income a month but he doesn't know that. I get to travel the world sometimes; I enjoy the memories of wedding, and baptisms, birthday parties, bridal showers, nature and more. I had a client that paid me an additional 5,000 if I traveled and stayed with his family for the weekend and captured priceless shots; it was that client that set off my business to be as successful as it is. I will climb a tree or lie in an ocean and get completely wet if I can get a good shot. I love what I do.

Bradley has gotten use to my travels, that's why when I told him that I had an important shoot this weekend that I couldn't reschedule he didn't argue with me. He wasn't excited that I was going to miss his sister's party but he understood. Bradley isn't Shyann's real dad; her dad was murdered before I gave birth to her. I met Bradley shortly after having ShyAnn and he insisted on taking care of her as if she was his own. ShyAnn is only 6 years old right now and she believes in her heart that Bradley is her father. I haven't decided if or when I would ever tell her the truth, she loves him so purely I don't know if I want to destroy that.

Once I placed my bags in the trunk of my SUV, checked my gas tank which was full, kept two bottles of water and chewing gum at my disposal for the ride on I was on I76 going toward upstate New York. I called his phone and he didn't answer so I left a message "Hey Wolfe, it's me Lacy I'm in route give me a call when you can".

My heart always race when I hear this man's voice. I didn't have a shoot this weekend, this weekend I was going to meet a man that has been my lover for the past year. I have always been faithful to Bradley but the constant routine love making was starting to bore me.

I mean Bradley was satisfying in bed but our love making always had to be in the bed. Year after year it was the same thing, I even wanted to have sex in the car one night after we came from the movies and he couldn't get erect. I was confused and angry. He said he was uncomfortable doing it with me like this. I shrugged it off as if it was okay but within me I was furious. Bradley was a good man by right so I went along with the way he wanted to have sex and whatever made him comfortable until the day I met Wolfe.

Traffic was inching along the freeway and my phone rang which threw me out of my thoughts. It was Wolfe "Hey sexy" Wolfe said with his deep voice.

"Hey babe, where are you?" I said feeling excited.

"I'm in route to my last shop to pick up this money, and then I am headed up there", Wolfe said.

"Oh okay", I stated sadly.

"What's up with you Lace, why you sound sad baby this is our weekend together I thought you would be a little more excited?" Wolfe asked.

"No baby I am good, just stuck in some traffic is all. Did you get the seafood yet"?

"Yes I did, 4 whole lobsters, 4 lbs of jumbo shrimps, and a sack of crab legs all seasoned just for you sweetheart", Wolfe laughed.

"Great so I will see you soon then", I stated trying to make my happy voice.

"Yeah babe I will call you when I'm close, is it anything else I need to get before I get there?" Wolfe said.

I thought for a moment and found nothing I could think of, "no, that's about it. Everything else will be delivered to the cabin".

"Aight then I will see you soon baby girl", I smiled and hung up the phone.

The feelings of excitement and turmoil all ran across my heart. Wolfe was the man, the man I wanted all my life. He was from the street, a true hustler indeed. Everyone knew him, he was intelligent and with this exquisite swag to him. He could talk to anyone and his business smarts was intriguing to me.

Wolfe owned six barbershops each one is as successful as the other. His father had a shop when he was growing up and kept that shop going; when his father died he left the shop to Wolfe and his brother Kem. When Kem was locked up, Wolfe took the business over but keeps his brothers share in a bank account so that when he gets out there is no struggle. Wolfe was able to combine his street smarts with business intellect and open shop after shop. He said when you hustle the street life long enough; it just takes money and some common sense to run a business properly.

I've been to every one of Wolfe's shops, with each one being neat and well organized. The young barbers all have their stations immaculate. There are flat screens in each shop so the guys can enjoy the games on game night and videos which plays when no games are on.

Wolfe put dollar soda machines that carry juices and water for his customers. Each shop has a kid's room so that when kids come in they don't have wait impatiently in the area, they can play until it's their turn which I thought was a brilliant idea. Wolfe has all his barbers meet together once a month to talk about how each shop is running and how the business can be better. Every month there is a training to upgrade each barber on the latest equipment, and techniques. Wolfe takes each lead barber with him to hair shows, and networks to find out the latest technology to see if it's worth its investments.

Each of his shops has annual BBQ's in the summer to give back to the community. Any where Wolfe goes, he is recognized. Community boards have presented him with trophies of the best small business owner in all Boro's. Wolfe takes all of that and leaves it at his mom's house. His mother is his heart, after Wolfe's father died, his mother was lost Wolfe explained to me one day. It took months before she would even eat a full meal. Once her mourning was over, Wolfe promised his mother that he would always take care of her. And then Kem getting arrested took another toll on his mom, so he makes sure she has the finest of everything and she's comfortable.

The traffic was finally moving again my phone was ringing again, this time it was Bradley I took a deep breath before I picked up the phone.

"Hello".

"Hey Lacy how's it going for you, we haven't heard from you in awhile I was just checking in making sure that everything was okay", Bradley said.

A tinge of guilt cut across my heart, "I'm so sorry Bradley, yeah I got caught up with a lot of things while I was packing, but I'm on the road now and everything is ok, how's Shy doing?"

"Ok, well I'm glad that you are okay, Shy is fine she's playing with the other children in the game room, and having a ball", Bradley said.

"How is your sister and the rest of your family doing?" I asked.

"Everyone is doing fine, it's just chaotic people in and out a lot of trips going back and forth to the airport, a lot of food deliveries, I mean it's just a lot going on but all for the good", Bradley said.

"Oh okay well I'm glad all is well at this time, please have Shy call me later before she goes to bed Bradley I want to speak to my baby", I said with a smile.

"Not a problem sweetheart, we'll call you later tonight", Bradley said.

"Okay we'll talk then", I said before hanging up.

The ripple of guilt ran through me even now more. I was dead wrong and I knew it. I was torn between two men. I loved Bradley but I wasn't in love with him. Wolfe came along and knocked me off my feet.

Wolfe tells me all the time to leave Bradley he wants to be with me, he said he would take good care of me and ShyAnn but I don't need a man to take care of us. I told Wolfe to give some time to think, I mean I have only been with him for a year compared to Bradley's dedication to me for over five years. It wouldn't be right to just leave him like this...I have too much to lose.

Bradley is the only man that ShyAnn has ever known as a father. I don't want to interrupt that. Wolfe understands and that is why we agreed that we will just see each other when we can until we can figure things out. I know that Wolfe has women at his beckon call so getting pussy for him is no problem. That is what makes me believe that he really cares about me, I always ask Wolfe why me? And his answer is, why not you? He told me that I am gifted and a breath of fresh air. He said he never seen anyone so passionate about what they do. His stated that his father was the last person he saw so dedicated to what he did for a living.

I reached into my bag carefully to pull out my pack of gum, and my heart started to thumb hard when my hand accidently touched the pretty envelope that I had written for Wolfe. The letter was probably the hardest thing that I had to write. The letter was the end of Wolfe and my relationship. It's probably the most selfish thing I have ever done. I agreed to come to the cabin with him in whom he thinks we are going to have this nice romantic weekend which we will; he just doesn't know it would be our last.

I didn't know how else to end it, I am in love with this man. I wanted to taste him and feel him one last time. I wanted to make memories with him. I wanted to feel him inside of me one last time. I wanted to watch him smile at me. I wanted to run my fingers through his soft hair. I wanted him to bite my shoulder gently which turns me on so much. I wanted to feel him lick my pussy so good, no man has ever gone down on me like Wolfe, it's as if he was born to do just that, he knows where to lick what to bite, and what to suck in a rhythm that brings me to a climax in a very short time. I was getting wet just thinking about his love making. His body is strong and he always stays in control, I have never known a man that knows exactly what they want and goes out and get it.

Wolfe is always teaching me things about life, telling me how I can better my photography business. When I am with him I am complete. I feel as complete as a woman can feel. His love is like a drug to me, when I tell myself that I am going to leave him alone, I always go back.

I tried leaving Wolfe several times in the beginning and he would let me be. The one thing about Wolfe he tells me all the time that he don't chase pussy. I would let weeks go by without calling or texting him and he would not attempt to call me. He knew my situation and said he wasn't going to disrespect my household until I gave him the word that I wanted him and not Bradley. I thought he was bullshitting but he stuck to his word. And before I knew it I would send that text message and we would be fucking in a five star hotel that night. I was addicted to this man's love. But I had to let him go before my whole world came crumbling down. I pulled in front of the cabin and the memories hit me like bricks again.

*****

Wolfe brought me here two months after we started seeing each other. He put a blind fold on me and promised me to not remove it. He told me that I had to trust him; he didn't have to tell me that because I did trust him. When I'm around him there is something about him that makes me feel so safe. I never told him that, and I never will.

When I came out of the truck he walked with me, I heard birds chirping, and water running like a waterfalls was close by. I smelled wood and fresh air. I heard him open a door, and that's when he took the blind fold off. I was standing at the door in an updated wood cabin that looked like it was in a magazine shoot. Everything in the cabin was brand new, and the smell of fresh wood was enticing. — *I can smell the cabin*

On the left was a huge kitchen with a double door refrigerator and all appliances was stainless steel. It has double sink and a top and bottom stove. On the left was a sitting room fully furnished with plush burgundy couches and a matching area rug and a fireplace with extra wood on the right of the fireplace, a big bay window was in there which sent sun light through the room.

Next to the sitting room was a lavish game room, with a pool table, fully stocked bar, a 50 inch screen flat screen TV, double recliner chairs, four candy machines filled with M&M's, Skittles, bubble gum, and starburst. All of my favorite candy, next to the game room was the master bedroom with a California king bed, a walk in closet, and a his and her bathrooms. A Jacuzzi sat on the right side with different bubble baths and fragrances all around it. The curtain in the bedroom was plush as if I could have taken one down and just wrapped myself in it.

"What is this"? I asked Wolfe with tears in my eyes each room that I walked in I was more and more shocked.

"This is our getaway baby", Wolfe said while holding me from the back.

"What"? I asked confused with tears in my eyes.

"I brought this cabin for us baby, I got a real good deal on it and sat down with an architect and redid the whole cabin to my liking just for us". Wolfe kissed my forehead.

"Wow", was all I could say at that moment no one has ever done anything like this before for me. All the food that was in the kitchen was all the things that I told him that I like. All the colors in the cabin were my favorite colors that I discussed with him. All the people that I told him I loved and honored were hanging on walls in each room, Bob Marley, Marilyn Monroe, Michelle and Barack Obama. I was in awe.

I remember standing there in the bedroom for the first time with so much anxiety and excitement. I started to take Wolfe's clothes off slowly. He didn't stop me. I was kissing him slowly and passionately. His moans were turning me on even more. I started to play with myself in front of, I sat him in the chair with only his boxers on, he wanted me the look in his eyes was alluring.

"No", not yet I said as I took my pants off nice and slow. I started rubbing my titties through my shirt and bra and moaning while looking straight into his eyes.

"Damn baby" Wolfe whispered while rubbing his erect, large dick.

I stripped myself naked and continued to play with myself on the bed, my toes were polished red and my legs were freshly shaved. And my pussy, well it was bald as a baby's bottom. I rubbed it and rubbed it until it was fully wet; I inserted two fingers in and squeezed my right nipple gentle for more pleasure, all the while not taking my eyes off of Wolfe. Wolfe was smiling like he was the cat that caught the canary all the while still rubbing his dick.

"You like this baby"? I asked him in between myself pleasuring moans.

Wolfe shook his head up and down nice and slow. Wolfe started to get up and come to me on the bed, "Oh no not the bed baby go sit on the couch over there", and he did as I commanded.

I strutted over to him naked took his boxers off and started sucking his dick with all that I had in me.

His moans were elevating in sound; "Oh shit" he would say every 30 seconds. I was looking as his face in between the licks of the head of his dick. I spit on his dick to moisture it and his legs went straight, "Damn baby you going to make me cum".

"And that is exactly what you're not going to do baby", I lifted up and whispered in his ear. Wolfe was breathing deep breaths now, not knowing what my next move was going to be. I strutted over to where the blindfold was laying and picked it up.

"Oh hell no Lace... not the blindfold", Wolfe pleaded.

"SHhhhhhhhhhh", I said to him, "If you want Lacy to finish off what she started you must let Lacy do things her way, understand?"

Wolfe didn't like not being in control, which turned me on even more. He gave me my way but not because he wanted to but because he loved sex, especially the different type of sex that I give.

"I promise you baby that it will be worth it", I whispered in his ear before sucking his ear lobe gently and stroking his dick. I placed the blind fold on Wolfe and he stood still, he wasn't relaxed so I gently started to suck his right nipple gently which he loved and gave the left nipple just as much love. He moaned that moaned that turned me on even more.

"Yeah baby just relax, you wanted me to trust you, now I need you to trust me". I whispered in his ear.

I went back down to his delicious dick and started sucking it again, this time with more aggression, Wolfe almost collapsed when I felt the blood rushing more, I fell back and started gently massaging it again.

"Don't cum baby, not now" I instructed in my sexy voice.

Wolfe let out an exasperation of pleasure, "Damn Lace what you doing to me baby?"

"Giving you all of me", I said seductively.

I climb on top on Wolfe now and placed his dick inside of me, it was so good to feel him in me. Wolfe moaned, "You like that baby?" I whispered in his ear

Wolfe moans told me he did, up and down I rode him in a rhythm, I took his hands and placed them in the curve of my hips, and he licked his lips and moaned in pleasure. I fucked Wolfe good, so good that I started to cum I felt myself climaxing and my pussy was getting wetter and wetter, I screeched out an outlandish moan. I wasn't finished yet. I took Wolfe out of my pussy and gently rose up some to place his large penis in my asshole.

"What are doing Lace"? Wolfe asked out of breath like he was doing all the work.

"I want you to fuck me in my ass while I'm on top of you, baby "I stated.

There was a silence, as Wolfe sucked both of his lips in and I knew that I had him now.

Wolfe lasted longer than what I expected in my asshole that night, but when he bust his nut every squirrel and chipmunk in close radius heard him. I took the blind fold off Wolfe and started kissing him deeply; he wrapped his large arms around my naked body. We sat there for what seemed hours before getting up and taking a nice hot shower together.

19

A red pickup truck rolled up behind me and took me out my thoughts; it was Mr. Willis the ground keeper for the cabin. He came by to make sure all the electricity and plumbing worked. He made sure we had no issues; I met him our last visit to cabin when the lights went out, and he came in and fixed them so fast I didn't know he left. Wolfe gives him great tips for coming by beside his pay so he is always efficient. When Wolfe and I started having sex and he brought the cabin, we were here every other weekend.

"Hey Miss Lady, glad to see again" Mr. Willis said as he came up to my side of my SUV, "Is Wolfe around?"

"Not yet Mr. Willis, he's on his way though", I said.

"Oh, okay well I'm going to go in and check out everything, hopefully he's here before I go I want to make sure you guys have a safe stay with no worries", Mr. Willis said with a slight smile.

"And we are grateful for that always Mr. Willis, I just got here a few minutes ago my bags are still in the back, do you mind taking them in for me", I asked.

"Anything for a beautiful woman as you", Mr. Willis smiled while tipping his cowboy hat that was covering the bald spot in the middle of his head.

I jumped out of truck and took in the fresh air, it was in the 60's this time of year it was springtime, but dropped in the 30's at night. I had my camera in tow and started taking pictures of the beautiful scenery before me.

I went into our bedroom where Mr. Willis placed my bags and started unpacking. Each time that I walked into the cabin I was reminded two things one that a man cares enough for me to create such beauty and two I was being deceitful to my life as I knew it. I looked around the cabin feeling bitter sweet knowing that this would be my last time here. Thoughts of other woman coming into this place and enjoying its pleasures made my stomach hurt some. It was my choice, I started this and I had to finish it.

I didn't want to leave Wolfe, I loved him but I couldn't go on living life like this. I had a daughter to think about, and although I would give my life for ShyAnn, the hungry sexual appetite I had for Wolfe seemed to overpower that in a sad way. How can something that feels so right, be so wrong? I needed a drink so I went to the bar and poured a glass of coconut vodka, with pineapple juice to help my thoughts.

Once Mr. Willis left, I gave him a tip he assured me that Maria that cleans the cabin will be here in the morning to give a cabin a thorough cleaning. She was suppose to come yesterday but had a family emergency. He also assured me that the delivery of food and other things that Wolfe ordered should arrive shortly at the cabin and for me to not get alarmed if a car rolls up.

By this time Wolfe still didn't make it there so I decided to take a hot shower and relax on the bed until he arrived.

Hours later

I felt kisses on face coming out of my sleep, when I opened my eyes it was Wolfe bent over me looking like new money. I smiled, and he kissed him passionately.

"Hey baby girl", Wolfe said all the while looking me in my eyes and rubbing my hair.

"You smell good baby-girl"

"Thanks baby, what time is it"? I asked confused at the lost of time since I went to sleep.

"It's a little after 7".

"And you're just getting here?" I asked.

"Nah baby girl I been here for awhile but when I came in and saw you sleeping, I let you sleep; you looked so beautiful laying there I didn't want to disturb you so I went and started watching the game", Wolfe said with a warm smile.

I sat up and looked at Wolfe, he was so handsome. He always had a fresh haircut, and I never seen him wear the same outfit twice since we met, his hands and feet are always manicured. He took good care of himself. His goatee was so sexy and skin was so smooth. I wasn't a flashy dresser like Wolfe was, but when it was time to go out I pulled myself together pretty well.

I put my feet on Wolfe and he started rubbing my feet and legs it felt like heaven.

"Have I ever told you that you have the prettiest feet and legs I have ever seen on a woman Lace?" He asked seductively.

"Every time you see them Wolfe", I blushed.

Wolfe was fully dressed with a crisp pair of jeans on and a polo shirt but his sneakers were off his socks were crisp white; he jumped on the side of me and held me so tight, "Talk to me baby girl," Wolfe said as he kissed my cheek.

I turned to him and started to rub his hair, I took in every detail of his face his eyebrows were thick and his eye lashes were longer than most women I knew. His lips were full and his nose was straight like a white man's but broader. His coco brown skin was flawless, he had high cheekbones and his face came to a point, that's where his strong features come from. I sketched my index finger around his whole face, he closed his eyes.

Wolfe took that same finger and started sucking on it. I started smiling, "You trying to read my mind Lace", Wolfe asked with a smile on his face.

"Why you ask that?" I said.

"I don't know, it seems like every time you do that it's like you are deep thought about me, trying to figure out my thoughts", Wolfe said.

"No Wolfe just thinking, thinking about us", I said sadly without realizing.

Wolfe gently grabbed my chin for me to look him in the eyes, "Lace, listen baby-girl we good right? I haven't felt this way for a woman in a long time. You know I want all of you but you know it's not my place to make that happen. You are the one in the situation so as a man I have to play my position. I don't like being with you like this, but I understand that this is the only way

I can have you, so I would rather have some of you then none of you".

My stomach felt like it did a back flip, I was looking in this man's eyes and feeling every word he spoke to me along with the guilt of my decision to let him go by the end of this weekend.

"Your eyes look sad Lace, something you want to talk about; you know you can tell me anything?" Wolfe asked.

"No baby, I'm good why you don't start running the Jacuzzi so we can get in and have some fun", I sat up and Wolfe was now over me like he was doing push up's, he licked my lips and it sent shock waves through my body.

"Now you see that's what I love about you Lace, you love to fuck and you're so damn sexy about it", Wolfe said causing me to blush.

Wolfe and I sat in the Jacuzzi with our drinks in our hands as I filled him in on Mr. Willis coming by and about Maria coming by also. I sat in front of Wolfe and felt his dick rising minute after minute. He was kissing my neck now, and we began to fuck like rabbits in the Jacuzzi.

As I was coming out the bathroom from moisturizing and putting on my T shirt and panties Wolfe was on the phone, I saw him go to the front door open it the cold air ripped through the cabin and gave me a chill. I walked into the kitchen and Wolfe was on the phone while taking plastic out of the bags putting food on the prettiest ceramic plates I ever saw. Wolfe blew me a kiss, and I caught it in the air and he smile and shook his head.

The cabin was really warm, Wolfe hung up the phone came over and kissed me on the lips, "Eat up baby girl, we worked up an appetite", Wolfe winked.

"Where did this food come from?" I asked looking surprised.

"You know I have connections baby girl, it just took a phone call, and you know yah boy got skills like that", Wolfe stated laughing, and as always he never misses a beat, it was my favorite fresh Salmon, steamed broccoli, with seasoned red potatoes.

"No but for real Wolfe, it's nothing in these parts for miles, who the hell brought us hot food at night up here?" I asked curiously.

"Well if you need to know girl, Mr. Willis wife made this especially for us. When I told him we were coming he asked if it was anything additional he can do, and he always brags how good of cook his wife is so I put the order in then and he assured me that he would have someone drop it off to us for dinner, and as you can see he is a man of his word", He said.

I looked at Wolfe with a smirk of pleasure, I was thinking this man never cease to amaze me, "Ok then Mr. Wonderful what is it, that you can't do?" I asked with a smile and my folk of salmon.

"Have the woman that I adore exclusively", Wolfe said in all seriousness.

My heart thumped at that moment, I saw sadness in him that I haven't seen before, "That's not funny Wolfe".

"I didn't say it to be funny, you asked me a question and I answered it".

I got up and went over to sit on his lap; he was angry but couldn't resist my love for him. I started to kiss him all over his face, he closed his eyes."You know, you are special to me Wolfe. We're like soul mates that met at the wrong time is all", I said as laid his head on my chest.

"I love the smell of you Lace", he said, making me smile.

We left that subject and finished up the food, it was incredible. I went to the bedroom to call ShyAnn and Bradley. Wolfe gave me my space, he knew if I was on the phone it was either a client or Bradley so with that understanding he never invaded my space.

"How's mama's big girl doing tonight?" I asked ShyAnn with excitement.

"It's really fun mommy, I won all the games of UNO", ShyAnn said.

"I'm sure that you did Shy, you're the best UNO player I know", I said with pride.

"Yes, I am mommy" she said confidently. "When will I see you again mommy?"

"Well in two days we will meet up again and how about we get your favorite ice cream cone from the parlor on Justin Street", I answered.

"Yes, my favorite, okay mommy we are going to watch a movie now I love you".

"I love you too baby, I will call you tomorrow".

Bradley and I said good night and I hung up the phone with deep sadness in my heart.

I was here with a man that made everything seem perfect, yet I wasn't being honest to anyone at this point. Wolfe and I agreed on these terms of secret escapades, and now I was ending it because I wanted to get my life back in order. It seemed so unfair to him, but I am engaged and seemed unfair to lead

Bradley on and marry him when I wasn't in love with him. I needed a drink fast; when I went to the game room Wolfe already had my drink made as if he could read my thoughts. I drank it down within seconds.

"Everything okay?" asked Wolfe with a corona in his hands.

"Yeah, everything is fine Wolfe just a lot of things coming up with work is all", I stated dryly.

After several more drinks, Wolfe and I was completely naked laying the California King plush bed that felt like Heaven. I was lying on his chest and he was running his finger through my hair. I never felt so complete in my life.

"Lace I want to talk to you about something's" said Wolfe in a serious tone.

"Ok, shoot I'm all ears", I said.

"What is this we doing, and how long are we going to continue to do it"? Wolfe asked.

I raised my head and felt sick by his question; I didn't want to talk about this right now I didn't want to deal with the hard stuff. I just want to lie in his arms and feel safe. "Wolfe we talked about this baby, it's complicated you know that I didn't know we was going to get to this point, I mean it's just so complicated".

Wolfe took a deep breath, "This isn't about sex to me anymore Lace, it's not. I care for you I do. We are cheating ourselves living this way. I mean I enjoy it, but I want more baby… I can give you the world, you know I can".

"Wolfe I know what you can do baby but this isn't about you and I. I have my daughter to think about, you know this. Bradley is the only father she ever knew how can I take that away from her now? I mean what if I leave Bradley and you and I don't work, then I would drag my child through hell and I'm not ready to do that to her Wolfe, just give me some more time to figure things out please".

Wolfe didn't respond to me, he just continued to rub my hair. I knew his silence was a sign of his pain. I felt even worse at this point. Tears weld up in my eyes I was torn and hurting. I deserved this pain because of my choices. But everyone I love I am hurting them. I had to end this with Wolfe it was the only way to mend these broken pieces.

We fell asleep peacefully…

I woke up to the smell of bacon and eggs, I heard talking coming from the kitchen. I went to the bathroom and when I went to my top drawn for my pink robe a framed picture of Wolfe and I was lying there in an 8X10 frame. I took this picture of us months ago, the frame was expensive we was smiling, we are happy. I took the frame out and stared at it for what it seems an eternity.

"I see you found it" asked Wolfe standing at the door of the bedroom.

"When did you do this Wolfe, it's beautiful"?

"I know a guy that owns a frame shop that did it for me as a favor; I thought you would like it being that you love pictures so much".

"You thought right baby, thank you so much".

I gently placed the frame on our dresser went to Wolfe and kissed him deep. He rubbed my back gently.

"Maria is here she made us breakfast after cleaning up come and eat, I have a great day planned for us".

We got back to the cabin before night fall, we drove into town and Wolfe set up a day of fun. We went horseback riding I never did that before. It was extremely fun. I took magnificent pictures of the horses we rode. I don't go anywhere without my camera. I was lucky to catch a male and female horse nose to nose. The picture was priceless.

I caught a few more shots of horses eating hay, a blue bird on fountain, and an eagle in the air was my favorite picture. Once I captured that one I was so excited I did my little dance in which I thought no one would see. Wolfe was watching me all the time, I never paid attention to him because I too engulfed in the shoot. Wolfe was smiling at me with his arms crossed; he had a look of pride on his face that dad's give their children. I blushed at my silliness and dancing and ran and jumped on Wolfe.

Back at the cabin it felt different to me, a bit cozier we lit the fireplace and indulged in a game of two man spades. I beat Wolfe all the time, sometime I think he just let me win. We then steamed the seafood I asked Wolfe to bring. The entire cabin smelled of old bay seasoning, and we drank Smirnoff ice coolers with additional liquor in them in our fancy his and her glasses.

The night was wonderful, the fireplace crackled and Wolfe and I sat quietly looking at it. Tomorrow we were leaving. I believe we were both thinking the same thoughts. We are both so unsure of our future, he more than I. The letter was in my bag, ready to be given to him. My heart was aching with the guilt and the shame I was feeling was overwhelming. I stayed quiet; silence is sometimes our greatest communication.

I loved Wolfe, I was in love with him I wanted him. I wanted to cook for him and cater to him. I wanted him to meet Shy and love her like I do. I wanted to meet his family and become a part of his life. He offered it to me, and I declined it. Its women out here that will die to have a man like Wolfe that thought upset me but it was the truth.

After taking a hot shower together, Wolfe dried me off and lotion every part of my body. I stood in the mirror and watched my coco brown skin glister with every motion of his hand. My light brown eyes reflected off the mirror; inherited from my grandmother Gene. ShyAnn is also blessed with these chestnut brown eyes.

My body was tight. I wasn't the typical big breast, round hip, big booty black woman. I worked out four days a week and I was more toned than fleshy in my 5 foot 1 inch frame. My legs were really thick and my waist was really small another great gene I picked up from mother's side of the family. The hair in my head was all mines it drifted right past my bra strap full and thick that is thanks to Sasha she is my Dominican hair stylist that brings back all sorts of deep conditioners from the Dominican Republic that grows the heck out of my hair. Most people think it's a weave but it's all mine.

He lotion my legs and feet, then Wolfe sat me on the edge of the Jacuzzi. It was cold against my ass but once he opened my legs and started licking my thighs I knew this was going to feel good. Wolfe mastered my body like no other man did. He took his time to please me. He licked every part below my waste, I mean every part. My head was straight back my toes were curled. It felt so damn good.

I didn't want it to stop as he licked my clitoris slowly and gently, licking my walls like lollipops. This went on for what it seems like forever, I grabbed his head my legs are in open scissor position and I am laid on the back of the Jacuzzi, all the bubble bath and luxuries scents have fallen to the floor, the lights were dim and I felt like I was going to explode in his mouth, but I didn't want it to end so fast.

I knew in my heart that this was the last time that I was going have my pussy eaten this good, my physical body was feeling so good but my mental was out of place. Tears started to roll down my face, in that instance Wolfe sucked apart of my clitoris that made all the juices in me come out, I screamed loud enough for the town miles away to hear me, my stomach tightened sweat dripped down my brow I was weak, my legs collapse on Wolfe's shoulders. I was out of breath from the joy that orgasm caused me. Wolfe continued to kiss my navel and small pecks on my stomach and up until he laid his head on my right breast.

"Was it good baby girl"? Wolfe asked. I couldn't answer him my mind was in a million places, "Hey Lace, you okay"?

"I'm fine Wolfe just gathering my thoughts after that pleasure" I half smiled.

"Come to bed now Lace, we have to get up early" Wolfe started to pick me up.

"Let me please you Wolfe" I begged.

"Not necessary I want to just hold you in my arms baby girl, tonight was for you now I might change my mind in the morning but right now I want to just hold you".

Once I gathered myself together I jumped in the shower again so that I was smelling fresh and clean for the man I loved. Wolfe and I talked most of the night about our lives, he told me that his brother will be getting out of jail next month and they was going to have a coming home party for him with no limits. His brother was charged for a robbery that he didn't commit, he was with the wrong people doing the wrong things at the wrong time and got caught up. His charges were dropped once the evidence was complete but his brother did serve over three years.

I told Wolfe about the up and coming shoots that I had coming up; he was always so interested in my work. He advised me on how I should navigate one of the shoots and I really appreciated his advice because I was confused on my vision for it. He was who I wanted to be with; I hugged him tighter tonight than usual.

I couldn't sleep when Wolfe fell asleep I slipped out the bed and started looking through some photographs that I shot recently. I put the pictures away and took the letter out of my bag. My plan was to put the letter in his carry bag that he takes with him everywhere, I knew that he would find it in there my hands started to sweat.

Tears started to weld up in my eyes, my mind flashed to Shy Ann's large smile, the way she made her cereal in the morning. I laughed out loud. I thought about Bradley and how good he was to us, at times Bradley seemed so disconnected to me. Some nights he would come home and we would barely say two words to each other, and other nights he would come home and give extra special attention. I never questioned his high's and low's I just dealt with it because I was too engulfed in what I was doing.

I started to realize that his late nights were becoming more frequent certain times out of the month but I could not stand in my glass house and start throwing stones at him. With the distance between us I needed love, Bradley neglected me with love…I was horny and craved attention.

Wolfe gave that to me and more. It was kind of lighter not having him in the house, not a lot of pretending had to be done. I mean when he showed affection it was out and open. But when he checked out, he checks out completely. Bradley is bent on showing his masculinity through paying all of the bills, so I have been able to have almost a half of million dollars in my savings account.

I asked him to let me at least pay the smaller bills but he insists that I put money away for ShyAnn's college fund. I never told him that my grandmother put over 20,000 dollars in college fund for ShyAnn before she died and by the time she reaches 18 it would have matured into more than enough money for college for her. I still have 1,000 dollars automatically deposited a month in our joint account to save face but Bradley doesn't know about my savings.

I was taught young that you never tell your right hand what your left hand is doing. Bradley was not yet my husband so I had to make decisions on what part of me I was going to reveal and what part I was going to keep to myself.

I watched Wolfe sleep and started to cry again. I took the letter and placed it in his bag underneath his clothes. He would have to take everything out before he found the letter. I closed his bag up properly went to the bathroom to wash my face. I crawled back in the bed with Wolfe and wrapped myself around him. He was warm, secure and safe. Once he felt my presence he cuddled me close to him. With my face away from Wolfe didn't tell him the tears that were coming down my eyes.' The man that I'm in love with will be no more'. I cried that night with a broken heart.

I arrived back at the house before Bradley and ShyAnn came home. I put my bags in the bedroom and started to make me a cup of tea. Lemon tea with two sugars was my favorite calming potion. I sat in my kitchen and looked around like I didn't live here. My heart was heavy.

The drive home made my heart race in a million directions. Half of me know that I did the right thing and the other half of me wanted to leave Bradley and go with Wolfe. I already made my decision so I had to deal with that. The love making Wolfe and I did this morning was making me almost change my mind. He handled me delicately as if he knew it would be his last. Our kisses were more passionate, his gazes at me were deeper. When we separated to our cars I said goodbye.

Wolfe his last words to me were always, "It's see yah later baby girl, goodbye means forever".

I just smiled and got in my truck. My heart was heavy.

"Hey hit me up later let me know you ok!" Wolfe shouted behind me, I threw my hand up in agreement, another lie I had to endure.

Bradley and ShyAnn came home about an hour later, I was so happy to see her that my heart melted. I was able to bring some souvenirs back from when Wolfe and I went into town; she loved everything I brought her.

Bradley looked fresh he wasn't the most handsome man in the world but his deep features made him more attractive. Bradley was 6'1, light skin with the nicest smile I ever seen on a man. He was thicker than Wolfe but maintained himself well. Bradley was an assistant director at Green bay Bank on 5th Ave. He has every color suit and tie you can imagine with matching socks and handkerchiefs. I asked Bradley if he ever wanted to have children his response was one day. It wasn't convincing to me so I stay on birth control until I feel otherwise. I want to give Shy Ann a little brother or sister but with my husband not just any man.

After we put ShyAnn to bed that night Bradley and I sat up talking in between the football game. I avoided as much eye contact with him as I could. He asks me several times what was wrong with me, I told him I was tired and had a long weekend, on little sleep. That lie seems to work. I was going through some photos when the game came back on. Although it wasn't a lot of conversation with Bradley and I, I sat around him enough to allow him to know that I wanted to be in his presence. I somehow convinced myself that if I look at him enough, or see him enough the feelings that I use to feel for him would come back. Day after day it wasn't working.

"So, I was thinking that we purchase the plane tickets for Layne's wedding in July this weekend" Bradley spoke all of a sudden.

I heard him but was looking at the picture of the horses and eagle that I took in town. Bradley was never interested in my work, only if I asked my opinion he would give it but besides that he would look and then look away.

"Lacy did you hear me"? He asked.

"Oh yeah that is a good idea, I will put a reminder in my phone when I'm done". I quickly answered.

"And make sure you use my credit card", Bradley reminded me as he did with every other purchase. I mean I wasn't complaining because I did appreciate having a man that wants to pay my way but it's the way that he said things that irks me the most.

I wasn't looking forward to going to his sister's wedding; although I didn't have anything against his family personally but they act too snobby for me. They were never rude to me in my face but the way they talked about people I just knew they had a lot to say about me. But his family embraced ShyAnn and treated her with more love then I expected, as long they love her there is nothing I can say. They buy her way too many things for no reason. And she loves to visit them.

I couldn't stop thinking if Wolfe found the letter yet. That chapter in my life was over. I had to accept it. I ached for Wolfe, I thought about our love making and started to take deep breaths, I closed my eyes. I ran upstairs to be alone. I couldn't escape the feelings I was having.

Bradley watched me go up the stairs but he didn't say a word. I peeked into ShyAnn's room and she was sound asleep a peace filled me to see my beautiful baby girl surrounded with so much serenity. I couldn't mix her life up right now. She wouldn't understand the decisions that I made to chose a man's love over her love. I wanted my daughter to have stability.

My childhood was nothing close to stable and I couldn't allow my child to endure the same suffering. In my heart I was doing the right thing as a mother, but a as woman I was depleted emotionally. I wanted a life that I couldn't have right now and I needed ShyAnn to feel the love that she had from Bradley and I being a complete family.

As a man Wolfe has shown me he has loyalty and dedication towards me and if I was single I would have locked Wolfe away with me a long time ago. Wolfe spoke sincere words but the truth is I can be blinded by his love. I know what he said but is he really ready to take on an already made family? I couldn't chance that with him now and our feelings are getting way out of control at this point. I closed her door gently went into the bathroom and cried my eyes out silently.

WOLFE

THE LETTER

When I got back to my place I dropped my bags off quickly. Sash and Pete was meeting me there to talk about what happen at my shop in downtown. After the weekend with Lacy nothing they were going to say to me was going to upset me. I couldn't get her off my mind. I wasn't comfortable with the way she started acting on our last night. There was something wrong with her, but she didn't want to tell me. I believe that once I offer my ear and you don't respond then my business is only what you want me know and nothing more. I sat on my recliner and flipped through Friday and Saturday's mail, nothing important.

My phone buzzed and I was hoping it was Lace telling me she was okay. It wasn't it was China asking when we would see each other. I put the phone down. China was sexy and beautiful half black have Korean and a body like she was straight from the south. When you look at her, you can see she has black in her more than Korean her curves were on point and her attitude too. She would curse you out at the drop of a time, real feisty. I kept her as my eye candy when we hit the clubs. Men drooled over her and I let them watch from a distance as long as they didn't touch.

China was good to chill with and she had my back. Whenever I called her for anything she came with no questions asked. She was managing my uptown shop for years and I trusted her with a lot. She showed me great loyalty.

Her sex game is average nothing to brag about but her loyalty is what keeps me connected to her. She was my number one chick until I met Lacy last year. Once I seen Lacy knew I wanted her, she was beautiful but her beauty was different. It was something about this woman that attracted me to her way before she said anything to me.

I remember when I first saw Lacy, Pete dragged me downtown to a live gallery where photographers and artist was showing their portraits. I'm from the street so when he first proposed it to me I was like no thank you this shit is too top shelf for me. Then he reminded me that these pictures were going to hang in our last shop we was opening on the south side and although I wasn't into art and pictures I wanted to have an say on what goes on my shops walls. My barbershops were like my babies I nurtured each one of them the same. I took my businesses seriously and sometimes as a boss you have to do things just for the sake of the business.

My driver dropped us off that night in front of the gallery. I knew by the line that was around the corner none of these people looked like us. But that didn't stop our mission. We don't stand on lines, so once Pete announced to the security who we were, the rope swung open and we were escorted in.

I heard whispers coming from the line. I assured Pete to remind the front desk that Karen and her sister was coming out tonight to give their opinions. Karen was my business partner, I trusted her with my life. We are childhood friends, everyone since we were teenagers thought we were fucking. But Karen don't like dick she's a lesbian and her girlfriend is prettier than most my man's girls hands down.

Karen is my ride or die; she is a great visionary and handles the books. A dime has never been short in any of my stores with Karen's expertise and sassiness. And if a problem arises she handles it and then lets me know how she solved it. She was like a sister to me; it's nothing I wouldn't do for her. She was the one to give me the idea to open up other shops after my pops died. I was too wounded to make a decision but with her aggressive nature we ventured off and here we are.

It must have been thousands of photos and pieces of art, although I didn't know what I was really looking at some of the

44

shots and art was nice. I separated from Pete when I saw camera lights flashing in the back. A live photo shoot was going on while the gallery was open season to the public. That is when I seen her, a coco beauty. She was relaxed with black yoga pants on, a red t-shirt, her hair was in a ponytail and her sneakers matched her shirt. She was focused.

I stood there in awe watching this woman direct and orchestrate this shoot. When she turned around I seen that her eyes were beautiful, they were round and light brown with a twinkle in them. I couldn't take my eyes off of her. I was use to half naked women parading around looking for the next dude to fill their pockets with money after they serve them the same pussy they gave their homeboy the night before. I knew the game and lived it day by day. What I was looking at was a breath of fresh air, she was different, she was beautiful, and she carried a confidence that I haven't seen the baddest chick carry in the clubs. I wanted her and I didn't care what it was going to take to get her.

"See something you like brother?" Pete crept up behind me to see what I was looking at.

"Beauty at its finest", I spoke low without looking away from this coco complexion colored queen.

"You talking about Shorty snapping the pictures in the red", Pete asked surprisingly.

"Shhhhh man I want to hear what she's saying to them".

Pete stood still for a moment, "Hey Wolfe, Shorty is cute but that's not your cup of tea man" shaking his head.

"No, she's not that, that is what I am admiring" I spoke quietly.

"Look over there at baby in the blue dress Wolfe, now she is bad as hell and she checking you out", Pete said casually.

"It's time for change player, these hoes out here only want whatever dude that will throw them money and take them shopping, I did that too much in my life; something new and different is what I am about now, when you grow up one day maybe you will feel that way too" I joked and Pete just sucked his teeth.

"Whatever you say boss", Pete replied.

I never looked away from brown eyes, and then she smiled and I walked closer to the shoot.

"Let's take a 10 minute Phil" she spoke to a white guy with dirty sneakers on and gray sweat suit

Everyone cleared the set. She was drinking a bottle of water looking at her cell phone as I approached the set; Pete went toward the front of the gallery.

"I see you like what you do young lady", I said.

She looked up; her eyes were more beautiful up close, "Oh yeah, and why do you say that"? She asked curiously.

"I see it in your eyes, I know passion and I see passion in you something my father taught me years ago", she stood up and walked over to me.

"Lassie Grant", she extended her hands to shake mine.

"Wolfe- it's nice to meet you", I extended my hand. Her hand was soft and her smile was prettier than her eyes

A reporter walked up to me to ask if I would do a story on community dedication, I gave them my card.

"So are you a celebrity? I'm sorry you don't look familiar to me" she asked confused.

"Not at all, I am just a business man"; I stated never taking my eyes off of her.

"So what kind of business are you in if you don't mind me asking?"

"Why don't you give me your business card and we can talk over dinner", I said.

"Wow, you hold no punches Huh? I'm not too sure about that but I will see you later after the shoot we can talk then", she stated with a flirty smile.

I saw an engagement ring on her left hand, it didn't distract me. I knew that whoever gave her that ring she didn't claim because her smile was too broad towards me. I didn't want to give up so quickly with her but the white guy came up to her.

"Excuse me, Wolfe was it? It was nice meeting you", and back to her passion she went just like that.

"Hey partner" Karen tapped my shoulder, "found a new friend I see".

"Yeah she's nice with what she does, just look at her", I answered.

"Okay Mr. Lover boy we here on business let's look around, have you seen anything you like"? Karen asked, scanning the room.

"Do me a favor K look around, find whoever deals with the sales here and tell them that I want every photo Lacy Grant has done", I said.

"Okay, and who is Lacy Grant may I ask"?

"That's not important, just do it please and I'm out", I said as I headed toward the front door.

"Wait Wolfe, where are you going we haven't decided anything"? Karen shouted behind me.

"Yeah I did just get those photos, have them sent to the uptown office no matter the price I have some business to take care of, any other pictures you think we can use buy them, text me when they get to the shop, I'm out".

Pete met up to me at the front door; he didn't question why the quick exit as we were waiting for my driver baby in the blue dress approached me. I let her down easy, told Pete to take her number for me my mind was on Lacy Grant.

Just when my driver was opening the door the white guy with dirty sneakers called me, "Hey Wolfe".

He was out of breath, he handed me a business card. I took the card and smiled; Pete just looked at me and shook his head.

The card said, 'Lacy Grant', Freelance Photographer and her business phone number, I flipped the card over she wrote her cell number on the back.

There was a knock on my front door that brought me out my thoughts, it was Sash and Pete. Sash was another business associate of mine; we hustled together on the streets back in the day when I opened my third shop I proposed for him to go and learn how to cut hair. It was like shoving food down a baby's throat but he did it and was great at it he actually mastered it and now he was my lead barber at the uptown shop.

Sash is one of the smartest dudes that I know. The streets call him pretty boy. His eyes were green and his workouts at the gym gave in a cut body that women adored. Sash was a player at heart, he moved through more woman than tampons. But he's one of the best barbers on my team. His clientele out beats any other barber I have no doubt.

I keep Sash close to me because he knows what the street wants and most of our clients range from the ages of 18-35, clients waits hours for Sash if they have too. I have watched it for myself so with him bringing my shop so much money I keep him close to me.

"Big Wolfe" Sash spoke as we fist hit each other.

"Wolfe, Wolfe," Pete chanted as he went straight to my refrigerator.

"So what's up with this situation"? I asked curiously as Pete and I sat down.

Sash and Pete filled me on what was going on at the downtown store. The advised me that the cameras caught one of barbers stealing inventory from the stock room. Things like toilet tissue and rags, small things but he's doing it often and they told me they fired him and waiting on two dudes they are going to interview to fill in his position.

I was in deep thought about this and I knew the young cat they were talking about the streets called him Man-Man. I believe he just had a baby, I know I gave a 1000 gift certificate to him for his baby shower that I was invited too but couldn't attend.

I was shocked to hear this about Man-Man he seemed like a good kid. I didn't share with Sash and Pete that I was going to go Man-Man myself to find out why did he feel he had to lose his job over petty theft? After we spoke a little more they left and left me alone in my thoughts.

Lacy was one freaky woman and I loved it. When you look at her she seems so innocent, so focused and she really is but what she serves in the bedroom out beat any woman I ever came across. Our escapades were great but my heart wanted more. I'm 41 years old now, time is ticking and I wanted to have children and start my life with someone. Lacy would be the only woman that I would do that with, and she is caught up in her situation right now which keeps me in the street and my options open to other women.

China texted me again, this time I responded. We agreed to meet at **"Leonard's"** it was a popular bar lounge in the village. The cabin love is always a good get away with the woman I'm beginning to fall in love with but the city life is what I know and love so to hit the street was always a good feeling. I sent Karen a text to fill her in and see what she knew about Man-Man, I told her to get me his address and any information about him I was going to pay him a visit.

I made it to Leonard's before China everyone in there knows me so I have my own table always reserved when I come in. The greeter at the door tonight was Jessica she was young but cute; I know she has a crush on me because she gets clumsy and nervous when I come into her presence.

When she walked me to my table I told her I was waiting for a friend, I gave her $50 tip. She was use to my good mannerism and grateful from the look on her face. When she walked off I couldn't help but look at her ass, it was tight and round. She was too young for my taste but if I was 10 years younger I would hit that just because.

A waiter came over quickly for my drink order; I ordered a bottle and keep my tab running for the night. China likes expensive things so I was going to cater to her wants tonight since I have been dodging her for a couple of weeks.

I couldn't get the thoughts of Lacy out of my mind, I missed her already but I don't go against code and call her. She knows to reach out to me when she wants to see me, but I am surprised that she didn't text me to let me know she was safe. That's not like her but I guess something came up. My thoughts were on the new shop we was opening on the south side, I had to get Karen to set several meeting so that we can have the construction companies finish up in order for our state inspection to pass. Kem is getting out next month, and the new shop opening I might have to hire an assistant on a temporary basis to dot some I's and cross some T's for me I will be sure to talk to K about that tomorrow.

Just as the waitress came back with the bottle and was in the process of opening it to pour it into my glass I saw China come strutting in looking bad as hell. I forget how sexy China is sometimes, but the mini skirt showing all her legs and black fish net stocking was enough to make any man look at her gay or straight. She has natural straight black hair that hung down her back with a bang in the front, her face was round and her lips was fuller than mine. She was drop dead gorgeous I was going to enjoy her tonight.

After banging China out real good back at my place I got up to check my messages and left her in the bed sleeping and I still haven't heard from Lacy. I returned a few calls and started to unpack my bag, I saw an unfamiliar envelope at the bottom of my bag. In neat writing the front of envelope read "Wolfe" in black marker? I opened it slowly

Wolfe,

This is the saddest thing I had to do since I buried my father. The joy you have given me in the past six months I couldn't describe in one word. The love that you give me is priceless. When I am in your presence the whole world is closed to me. You're on my thoughts daily; I breathe your scent even when you're not around. Your gentleness in unique and honest to me, every part of me wants to pack up me and ShyAnn's things and run straight into your arms. But I can't do that now. It's unfair to continue to love you only halfway.

I know your life doesn't stop for me, but our feelings are deeper than I was expecting and because of my situation too many people can get hurt from this. If I continue to see you as we do, I'm afraid that I am going to make unproductive choices only using my heart and not my head. We are in deep but not deep enough that we can't save ourselves a bunch of pain if we don't end this now. I know it was wrong to agree to meet this weekend and not just tell you this face to face but I was selfish and wanted to have one last time. I apologize for that, I really do. My intentions were to never hurt you Wolfe. When it comes to me, you are everything I ever wanted and desired, but for ShyAnn it's not and as a mother I must consider her feelings in this. I have been deceitful in ways that I never thought was in me, but you make me weak you brought my defenses down and I trust you as much as I love you. My heart is aching over this Wolfe please believe me.

You deserve a woman that can give you all of her and move on in your life. I don't want you to sit around while I am still trying to figure things out. It's not fair to you. I know women who would die to have a man like you in their life; it pains for me to say that but it's the truth. I know you are probably going to hate me for doing this, this way but please know that I didn't know any other way to do this. I can't look you in your face and tell you this; I am falling in love with you Wolfe.

It's best to part our ways now baby so that this pain don't continue to stir in me. My life will never be the same without you Wolfe, NEVER. And although I won't be around, you will always be in my thoughts.

I'm so sorry!

Lacy

I crumbled the letter up and swiped my dining room table with everything on it. The feelings that were in me couldn't be contained. My first thought was to call her ass up and talk to her. My second thought was to get in my truck and head over to her house and knock on her door.

I was pissed off, but none of that was going to make this situation right. My heart was hurting and this is why I never get my feelings caught up with females. I don't know what I was expecting, I guess I thought she would just up and leave her situation. Thoughts corroded my mind and nothing was sitting well with me.

What the fuck is she thinking, its other ways we can do this? I took some breaths, took a bottle of water out of the refrigerator and sat down. I didn't think of this as ending, I knew she was acting funny at the cabin but I thought it was about her family. I should have addressed it more. I should have not left that cabin until the Lacy I know came back emotionally. But my pride and codes stopped that. My own made up rules of the street prevented me to be open and talk to her about her behavior. I heard movement from my bedroom, I forgot China was here.

"Hey you" China stood butt ass naked at the kitchen door looking sexy as hell.

I didn't respond.

"Wolfe what the hell is the matter with you?" China snapped when she realized the things on the floor and the look on my face.

I blinked and saw Lacy standing there, and took a sip of water, "Oh so now the cat got your fucking tongue?" China spat.

I wanted to tell China to get the fuck out; I wanted to yell at her like she was Lacy. I wanted to her to gather up her shit and go, call my driver to pick her ass up. I wanted to be alone in my thoughts. Instead I put the water down and motioned for her to come to me. She did.

I pulled down my sweat pants and she knew it was time for her to suck me hard. The hot feeling of her mouth, with the long strokes of her hand was getting the job done. I didn't want to think about Lacy now. I wanted to erase her out my mind completely.

Once I was fully erect I pulled out of her mouth and pulled her up, pushed her over the table face down ass up, licked my two fingers to make her wet enough for me to enter her and stuck my dick in her from behind. I was pounding China out of full frustration. I didn't want this to be her, I wanted it to be Lacy as I thought it, I pounded harder.

The moans that were coming from China I barely heard over the frustration I was feeling in my heart. China was a freak she liked shit like this; she thought it was about her. I slapped her fat ass, she screeched.

I was angry and China's pussy was feeling my wrath. It was feeling good physically but mentally I was fucked up. As I felt myself coming I pulled out and came all over her ass, my legs were weak.

I gathered myself up and went to the bathroom, when I came out China was fully dressed on her way out the door. I didn't stop her; she looked at me with evil eyes and slammed my front door. I saw the letter that I crumpled up opened and lying on the table, I didn't give a fuck about her feelings at this point. I went to the bar and poured me a drink; it was early but "fuck it" there is no rules to drinking so I drank until I passed out.

I woke up with my head pounding and Karen standing over me with a confused look on her face. The crumbled letter in her right hand, I was laying across my couch too sick to get up.

"So you and camera girl got this serious and you are all in your feelings about this letter"? Karen stated like a mother scolding her child. I grabbed both my temples and tried to rub her out of existence.

"You look a mess", Karen said while walking away toward my bathroom, and then she walked to the kitchen. The clicking of her heals on my hardwood floor almost made me want to throw up.

"Try sitting up and take these", she instructed pushing a bottle of cold water in my direction, with 2, extra strength Excedrin. I smelled coffee brewing, I sat up swallowed both pills in one gulp and laid back down, Karen sat down on my coffee table directly in front of me, her hands was folded like I was kid in the principal's office.

"I don't want to hear this shit right now Karen, I'm not in the mood" I stated and closed my eyes.

Karen didn't respond she got up went to the kitchen and returned with my favorite coffee mug that I never use, and the matching saucer under it, "Here, sit up and drink this", she placed the coffee in front of me.

I sat up and took a sip almost spit it out, "What the fuck is this K?"

"Its black coffee, drink the whole cup nice and slow. This with the combination of Excedrin will take that headache away quick, and then I'll make you a bagel so you can get rid of that headache". She sounded like my mother for a moment.

I looked at her with exasperation and did as she instructed, I somehow felt a pinch of relief then I did five minutes ago.

"About time I finish telling you, what you need to hear that headache should be gone", Karen sat right back in her position in front of me. I was sipping the nasty beverage.

"Wolfe we cool and you know I love you like cook food, but I told you not deal with that female because of her situation, I saw it the first day at the gallery she was different not your usual cup of tea"

I bit my bottom lip not wanting to hear what Karen was saying because I know her truth was real but I had no choice but to listen besides the headache I was in a dangerous emotional state of mind. I needed guidance on this.

"Listen you know that I'm the last person in this world to tell you what to do, you know this but I'm a woman, camera girl wasn't about the glamour life she wasn't these hungry hoes out here looking for the next dude to take care of her finances, she is beautiful and talented, driven and attached in a situation that you clearly knew about".

Karen paused then continued, "Wolfe chicks like camera girl are not impressed by dudes like you friend, and that is what really attracted you to her beside the beauty she expels on the outside".

I stared at the floor and took another sip of coffee.

"I'm going to be completely honest with you Wolfe because I'm your friend and because I love you. You wanted to conquer her like all the other women, you set out to get her because your arrogance and pride thought that you could pull it off like all the rest. And with all the warning signs you didn't want to listen to me." Karen said confidently.

I looked her in the eyes now.

"Yeah I know you're mad and pissed off now, but I see my friend for the first time in his life hurt, big Wolfe that the streets know and respects. You're hurting because this one you didn't win", Karen said.

I took a deep breath, my headache was definitely getting better, and I pushed back and sat back on the couch looking straight ahead in my own zone.

"Wolfe there is plenty of women out here, and I know you that but for some reason we want what we can't have. I read this letter, as fucked up as it may seem that woman spoke her truth in it, she has a daughter to think about this is bigger than your sex life my friend".

"It's not about the sex anymore K, I'm feeling her period", I stately slowly, my head feeling like slow drums was beating inside of it.

"Exactly now you're feeling her but the sex was the first impulse, and when she served you better than your expectations you wind up here in this broken place".

I took a deep breath, and another sip of coffee it felt like every word Karen was speaking was curing my headache, "Come on Wolfe, you know emotions and feelings don't come with instructions. You broke many hearts in your life and now you're at the other end of it. Karma's a bitch sometimes friend", she said empathically.

"Now what"? I asked.

"Now you sit in these feelings, feel what you got to feel we call you Wolfe not Jesus, even he endured pain on this earth", Karen said with a chuckle. I had to smile at that one

"Then you can get off your sexy black ass and get back in the game man, you have businesses to run -people that depend on you. Kem will be out soon, a new chapter in life just let this be a lesson learned".

I sat the finished mug and saucer on the coffee table and folded my hands in front of me.

"Wolfe she loves you, I believe she does but you know that love is an emotion you can't live on that alone other elements come into play listen she let you go, you know the saying if she comes back then she's yours hands down. But for now life must go on, we got a lot to do friend".

As much as I wanted to shut Karen out, I knew she was telling me the truth and it hurt. My arrogance and pride put me in this position. When you have money you feel invisible, I have been so use to getting my way with women, Lacy shocked my system. I don't have children I could never understand the love she has for her daughter, I don't know her whole story. I love her and that's a fact but I know that I'm a man with great responsibilities and as much as my heart hurt I got to let this burn and keep moving. Lacy made her decision, I have to respect that and keep moving, I couldn't let this distract me from what I have going on.

"You okay there friend?" Karen asked as I came out of my deep thought.

"I'm good K, thanks for always having my back for real. Your right I got shit to do, if she wants me she know where I'm at let's just hope it's not too late".

"That's the strength I know talking now, when does your cleaning lady come this place is a mess?"

"It's on the calendar in the kitchen, if it's not today call the cleaning company have them send someone as soon as possible please", I said.

"Yes sir", Karen said as she stood up.

I started to get up from the couch slowly, "Your head is getting better right", Karen said with a smile.

"Yeah man, you are a genius K. I'm going to take a hot shower can you hook up a bagel for me too I need something on my stomach", I asked.

"You want me to scratch your ass too?" Karen said rolling her eyes.

"Nah I got that", I chuckled as I walked to the bathroom.

"And hurry up, we got business to tend to", Karen yelled behind me.

After my shower I felt much better I wasn't a hundred percent but I was much better. I owed Karen real big for nursing me back. Some of the words Lacy wrote in the letter haunted my thoughts but I didn't let them overtake me. Karen had my bagel ready when I came out fully dressed. We sat down and filled me in on everything. Karen assured me that all the shops was running smoothly, our profits are high and more and more customers are hearing about us since the billboard downtown was put up. That deal came from God, the councilman in my district made me a proposal that I couldn't deny.

One of the agreements was that the billboard of my shops with each shop address and contact on there. That lead me to open up this shop on the south side, it's not the wealthy side of town and we will shave off the price a couple of dollars because of the neighborhood, and we will give students an additional 10% off if they bring in any grade over a 90 in any major subject. It was our way of motivating education.

I usually visited each shop a couple of times of week, besides checking the books and talking to my lead barbers about any issues I always spoke with my customers. I engaged in the public, my father taught me that was important to do. You never get too big in life that you forget that if someone cut you, you will bleed blood just like anyone else. Those values he taught me never left.

Karen didn't have a lot to say about Man-Man she gave me the same information that Sash and Pete did; but she did give me his home address.

Once I left my crib, I took my BMW out my garage. I wanted to drive today I needed to clear my mind, and listen to some music. I made a decision to not think about Lacy, I knew if I did I would need to see her and that was not an option. She made her decision and it wasn't me.

I pulled up in front of the address that Karen gave me to Man-Man, the house was old, some siding was coming off of the house and the front yard had a grill and white chair sitting out. The garden on the left look as if someone was taking care of it. The green fence could use a paint job. I walked up and knocked on the door. A young female came to the door holding a baby; I assumed it was Man-Man's girl.

"Can I help you" she asked looking concerned.

"Hello, is Man-Man here?"

Before she could answer Man-Man came to the door, "Go back inside Gina, its' okay".

Man-Man was tall and skinny, look like a ball player he needed a haircut and he seemed like he was expecting me. He showed no fear but couldn't look me in the eye.

"Seemed like you were expecting me", I said to him.

"Not really" he stated dryly. We went to stand in front of my car; he was eyeing the car like it was a naked woman.

"Never be impressed by another man's possessions, it's all perishable", I said to him as my father used to say to me when I younger. Man-Man didn't reply.

"So you want to tell me what happened at the shop that you're not there anymore?" I cut to chase.

Man-Man took a deep breath and put his hands in his pockets while his head was down, "The cameras have you clearly taking these things, but why those things I'm confused Man" I folded my arms this time.

Man-Man was looking at my new sneakers hard, he slowly peeped my whole outfit before looking at me in my eyes, "Shit is rough out here Wolfe, money is tight I picked up a second job washing cars and needed some stuff to keep my work flowing, that's my word", Man-Man looked toward his front door.

"What's going on with your clients at the shop?" I asked.

"I mean I have clients but a lot of them aren't tipping so well, after paying for my booth it just seems like since the baby came it's never enough. Shit is hard out here Wolfe", he sounded agitated.

I was in deep thought, when I looked at his house I saw his girl looking out the window, "I could go back in these streets again and start slinging, but I got a baby now man I'm trying to live my life right now but it just seems like nothing is enough, the more I work the less is there", he started pacing back and forth slowly.

I saw the frustration in this young kid; I saw his struggle from where he lived, the envy in his eyes, and the sadness in his girls face.

"I respect you Wolfe I do, and I'm sorry man for stealing from you it was fucked up for me to do but I didn't have a choice. Now I'm even more fucked up now because not having my job at the shop just made shit worse for me", His head was down.

"Man-Man, always look a man in the eye when you speak to him", I said sternly.

He slowly looked at me in my eye, "Rather right or wrong never cut the hand that feeds you boy, NEVER! I'm at the shop at least once or twice a week you should have spoken to me about this".

He didn't respond

I took a deep breath, "I checked you out before I came here, I hear you a good kid and hardworking. I know your grandmother died last year and you have been in charge of paying everything. I know you owe the corner store on Brent Street $50 dollar credit. I also know that you go to church every Sunday with your baby and girl. I know that you help out at the veteran's center volunteering when you're not working because your uncle died in the war."

He looked me in the eyes this time and didn't look away.

"You seem like a smart kid Man-Man, and I see potential in you I want you to come to south side shop tomorrow at noon and bring your girl and baby with you".

"Is it something I should be worried about", Man-Man said confused.

"You'll know when you get there, don't come one minute late. And if you ever take anything else from me or any of my shops again both your hands will get chopped off", my tone was serious.

Man-Man looked at me and nodded his head.

"When you need something in this world trust to ask for it, it can save you a lot of trouble".

He nodded his head again.

"Noon tomorrow", I said and turned around to my car.

"Aight Wolfe", he said as he started walking away.

I took one last look at his house and seen his girl standing in the door with the baby in her arms, I stopped and went in my pockets, "Hey Man-Man, come here real quick"

He started walking back to me, I handed him a hundred dollar bill, "Buy your baby some pampers and milk".

He reached for the money, and took it slowly. He was confused but in need, he was grateful and hurt, "Thanks Wolfe".

"Noon, not a minute late", I said opening my car door.

✽✽✽✽✽

I arrived at the shop early, the inspection code passed for it with flying colors. The men were there installing the chairs to each of the stations. People from the neighborhood were outside looking at the new business in their area. The red and white floors looked dull from the dust of the workers but it was coming along nicely.

This shop should be open within two weeks which I felt good about. In the corner sat two of Lacy's photos. I wasn't going to put them up at first. But I loved these two photos and I didn't want to spite her. I loved her, I wanted her. I just didn't want any reminders of her. When I was fucking this white chick Lisa last night at her place, Lacy was on my heart heavy. I hurried up with that pussy, it was tight and moist but it wasn't Lacy. I knew I had to keep busy or I was going to do some foul shit. Pete was meeting me here by noon everything was in its right order. I hired a cleaning company to come in after the chair installation to mop and dust and shine everything. I need this place decent for when Man-Man arrived.

His girl walked in first, she was prettier than when I came to house yesterday. She pulls herself together well. The baby was asleep and Man-Man had a look of concern on his face but he quiet and didn't ask any questions. I had chairs set up for them, after showing them a quick glimpse of the shop.

"So I'm sure you're wondering why I asked you to come here today", I asked looking him in the eye.

His girlfriend seemed more concerned than he did with her facial expression, "Yeah, I won't front I'm a bit curious" Man-Man said plainly.

Pete and I looked at each other, "I brought you and your family down here today because I wanted to offer you the position as lead barber here, and if you do well after 90 days you can manage this shop under Pete's direction until you can master it on your own".

"Are you serious?" Man-Man asked then looked at his girl that was rocking the baby.

"Nah, I called you here today just because I ain't got shit else to do with my time, yes I'm serious", Pete said smiling.

"I'm confused", Man-Man said with his hands open.

"Look, you did a fucked up thing by stealing from me but your intentions was innocent. You have a new baby, you have experience loss from your grandmother, and you're a young man trying your best. You were taking towels and soap Man-Man but you were still paying for your booth and you could have taken money from the register and more valuable things, but you didn't".

His girl starting smiling and hugging the baby, as he continued, "Listen my father started out with nothing but a shop and with a wife and two young sons' he was a family man, he worked his ass off to provide for us. Sometimes you do things in this world because you want to but because you have too. You have a family to look out for, everyone deserve a second chance your dedication of hard works has been shown to me, I have connections around here I know".

"Wolfe I don't know what the hell to say", Man-Man's eyes was building up with moisture.

"Say thank you is enough", I said.

He came over to me and gave me hug, I saw a happy man, and he then went to his girl and kissed her and his baby.

"Listen, Pete is going to work out all the details for you. In this envelope is a little starter money for you I don't want you taking nothing else from anyone. Pete will mentor you, anything you need you ask him or me inside the envelope is my direct number never hesitate to use it, walk around the shop again feel it out", I said as I passed him the envelope.

"Wolfe man I can't thank you enough man, my family thanks you, you know I heard you do good by people but I thought it was just all talk. I'm grateful for this man", Man-Man said excitedly.

I saw a light of happiness in this young man. Yesterday at his house he was broken a sad and today I changed his whole life. My father use to tell me that it was nothing like being good to people especially when they are in need. I believe this young kid will do well because someone believed in him he has no choice, I don't give third chances.

"Thank you Mr. Wolfe", his girlfriend said with a southern drool and a big smile.

"Keep him in line", I said and winked at her.

"Pete I'm out, hit me up later", I said.

I felt good about what I just did which means I know I did the right thing, the fact of the matter is too many young black men out here is suffering. If I could offer that opportunity to every one of them I would but for right now Man-Man got that opportunity.

My driver dropped me off and once I walked into my house Lacy's face was all I could see. I haven't heard from her over a month. No text and no calls. She really made her decision, my ego was crushed I called China she hung up on me the first two times, the third time she heard me out. My driver went to pick her up.

LACY

RECONNECTING

Bradley was on an overnight business trip in Chicago, it was a relief to me because it's been hard balancing my emotions around him lately. He has been more distant lately, I don't know if I am responsible for this distance with him now. He catches me in deep thoughts when I'm not aware of it and each time I give him a different response. We haven't really been having sex like before. It's been two months since I gave Wolfe the letter and the summer is approaching slowly. I have been better than I have but I still ache for him. I look at Bradley sometimes and dislike him for being here, I wish he wasn't. I wish I could just have my way but I can't.

By Bradley being gone it gave ShyAnn and me time together, we are tight but she adores Bradley so I took her shopping to buy new summer clothes and I went to look at a couple of properties to open my own gallery. My clientele has picked up and I'm going to need help with the work I have booked. I remember Wolfe telling me how easy it can be getting space you just have to know what you want and where you want to be located. I have Mikey as my traveling assistant, he's a young kid with great vision and if I get the new space I will offer him a permanent position to work with me. I would also need to hire a secretary to handle all my appointments and other administrative things. It was sounding so good to me every time I thought about it and it took my mind off of Wolfe. Tonight Mrs. Krauss will watch Shy Ann for me my best friend Melissa asked me to go out with her and being that I am in a funk from all the events in the past two months I agreed to go.

ShyAnn and I was in the ice cream parlor, we sat in a corner booth her big brown eyes was so innocent and she was so smart, "Mama, can I ask you a question?"

"Sure baby you can ask me anything you like, shoot"

"Is it wrong for two men to be together?" ShyAnn asked.

I was shocked at her question; I didn't understand how or why she would ask a question at six years old. I was dumb founded, "Shy, why would you ask something like that, where did you even get that idea from?"

She shrugged her shoulders and took another scoop of ice cream, "I was just asking Mama".

"Is it something that you saw on TV?" I asked feeling confused.

She didn't answer me at first, "I asked you a question young lady", I said, speaking firmly to her.

"No mama, just forget it"

I wanted to forget she asked the question and didn't want to finish my ice cream at this point, "Shy Ann Elizabeth, if it's something you been doing or watching I need for you to tell me the truth right now".

"No mama... just some kids at school was talking that's all" she took more ice cream from her cup. That somehow made me feel a little better, kids with their explosive minds. It's scary to think the things they are exposed to.

"Mama, do you love Brad-Brad"?

Another question that caught me off guard, "Of course I do Shy. You know Bradley is very important to me".

"Important is different than love mama".

I was stuck with that one, "Your right, I love Bradley ShyAnn why would you ask that question"?

"Sometimes Brad-Brad seems so sad, when I ask him what's the matter he has the same look on his face that you do right now", she said so innocently. I didn't know how to respond

"Well sometimes adults have a lot of things on their mind and it's hard to keep inside our hearts so we may look sad sometimes like you do when you can't watch TV past your bedtime".

She thought about what I said, "Oh, okay I understand now", she smiled.

"The next time you see Bradley sad just give him a hug, hugs make people feel so much better".

"That sounds like a good idea mama, I will do that", she said sounding excited.

We finished up in the parlor and we went to look at some spots, I liked one location but I wasn't impressed with the other one. My realtor Jeff told me that he will keep me posted on any new listing coming up.

The drive home was heavy for me I couldn't get the thoughts of what ShyAnn was saying to me earlier. But I needed to clear my thoughts for going out tonight with Melissa; she was a firecracker and the most honest person I know. If it will hurt your feelings she will tell you, but she also encouraged and motivates me at the same time in all aspects.

I was scheduled to bring Shy over to Mrs. Krauss by 7:00p.m. that would give me time to get dress in peace. I can put my music on and just focus. I wasn't the dress up type of woman, I liked being comfortable with yoga pants or sweats on but since I left Wolfe I just want to feel sexy. Tonight I am going out of my element, I picked out a fitted all black dress, with the highest blue pumps I had in my closet. I matched some jewelry I had a let my hair flow. The season is changing so the nights are warm but not so warm that my hair will frizz up.

Once I was done and looked in the mirror I was impressed at how beautiful I looked. I would like to say I haven't been horny but I am not talking to no man tonight I am engaged and I will not create another emotional disaster. Tonight is about all fun, period.

Melissa and I was to meet up at a hall on Frisk Street by 10:00 pm, I found a parking spot and texted her to see if she was there yet. To my surprise she was, and gave me direction what to do when entering. The place was beautiful it was a five star hotel and top notch. As I approached the front brown people were standing outside, some was smoking cigarettes others were just talking. Everyone was dressed to impress so I felt better in what I had on. As I was approaching and a tall gentleman with fair skin and very handsome approached me.

"Hey beautiful, can I holla at you for a minute?" he asked rubbing both his hands.

His hands were nicely manicured, his teeth were white, and his height was nice I found myself looking up to him, "Oh, I am here to meet my friend, maybe later", I said politely.

I kept walking and heard other dudes squawking at me, it felt good to get the attention but I was focused on having fun.

"Remember you said that, love", he hollered behind me.

Melissa was waiting at the top of the stairs looking beautiful as always, Melissa was light skin with chink eyes. She was thick all over blessed with big breast and booty to match. She loved weaves and every time I seen her it was different one in her head. She was always put together so well I envied her style.

"Look at Miss Thang, damn girl you look wonderful" she said louder than I wanted her to say.

"You look good too girl, as always" I said while touching her new weave.

"Girl, there are so many men in here I feel like a kid in a candy store. And they are men too just big and brawly with money in the pockets".

I laughed at Melissa she was always so over dramatic, "So whose party is this anyway, the place is beautiful".

She and I walked towards a table and sat down, "Girl it's a friend of mine friend's party. I met him like two months ago, I know he's a player but he buys me whatever I want he has the prettiest green eyes and the sex is on point. When he invited me I was like hell yeah, it's free and all the drinks and food are too", she laughed.

I shook my head, "I hear that".

The tall guy from downstairs came toward me but was interrupted by a dark skin big booty female that looked like she wanted to devour him. I was glad she stopped him. He was nice looking and I just didn't want to get distracted.

Melissa and I went to the bar and got drinks, I like the taste of my coconut vodka and pineapple juice. I haven't drunk it since the cabin. It was inviting, as I was thinking about Wolfe sadness came over me. I drank my drink down real fast.

"Damn Lace, take it easy girl that was fast!"

"I'm going to get another one", I got up and walked over to the bar again.

This time while my drink was being made, the first drink gave me courage to look at the crowd. It was many black beautiful men and women in here tonight. Whoever's party this was had money for sure and taste. The decorations were all blue and silver. The tables were set up nicely, and dance floor was huge. I loved to dance and I was feeling like I wanted to start right now. I looked and saw a lady that looked familiar to me. I couldn't remember where I saw before but I know I knew her. She was at a distance.

Once I got my drink I was back sitting with Melissa, she was now talking to a nice looking brown skin man with an expensive watch on and thick lips.

I sat down, and smiled at her and lifted my drink in the air, "Can I have this dance" a familiar voice said to me.

I looked up and seen the handsome man from outside. I was feeling tipsy so I didn't think at all. I jumped up, "Lead the way"

He looked surprised, as slow song blurted through the speakers, which I didn't mind. He held me close and started a conversation; I gave him my name and what I did for a living he seemed like a nice guy.

Another slow song came on and we continued to dance. We were close, he smelled good and I was feeling those drinks. I started to get hot between my legs.

"Oh I see my brother now I heard him say", I ignored him and was just feeling the mood.

"I want to introduce you to my brother Lacy", my eyes were still closed but as I opened them Wolfe was standing before me and looked good enough to eat. I started to feel sick. Wolfe was looking at me with a blank look on his face.

"Am I missing something here brother?" the handsome one spoke.

I coughed twice, "This is Lacy Grant", Wolfe spoke looking directly at me.

My heart was palpating really fast, "Wolfe what are you doing here?" I slowly asked.

"This is one of my friends and business partner's party we are throwing for him", Wolfe spoke looking me dead in the eyes.

"Wait, this is the infamous woman Lacy?" the handsome one spoke laughing out loud.

I realized in feeling so tipsy I never asked him his name, and he never offered it. I looked toward the table and Melissa was eyeing me down and she started to get up and come towards us when she the look on my face.

"Lace is everything ok?" Melissa said while looking at Wolfe with lustful eyes.

"Um, yeah-Melissa this is Wolfe and I'm assuming Kem is your name", I stated looking at handsome.

Kem smiled at me, while checking Melissa out, "Beauty with beauty", Kem said as he gawking at Melissa.

"Well I'm going to leave you two to your dance", Wolfe spoke still looking at me.

I didn't know what to say, as he was walking away a beautiful mixed woman approached him with all her ass and titties out in a dress that looked painted on her. She looked me directly in the eye.

"Wolfe baby you ready to take our seats", she spoke confidently.

My heart dropped as they walked off, I wanted to run up to him and kiss him. I missed him so much.

"What the hell was that about?" Melissa said confused.

"I will tell you later right now I am going to finish my dance", I went to grab Kem but he pulled back.

"Whoa, you are one beautiful woman Lacy that's a fact but by the look on my brother's face I'm going to sit this one out. Blood first, I'm sure y'all will work this out".

I looked at him surprised, "Well okay then", I said and walked away. Melissa was right behind me.

"Ok girl I'm guessing that was Wolfe, oh goodness Lacy are you okay girl", Melissa said

"I'm good, I'm here now and I'm not leaving, I came out to have a good time and that is what I am going to have".

When I looked toward Wolfe he was talking to a few people that approached his table. He was an important man. People approached him wherever he went, "I'm going to the bathroom".

"I'm coming with you, just in case", Melissa was side by side walking with me.

I told Melissa about Wolfe from day one, I didn't speak to her about the letter and the ending. I filled her in quickly in the restroom and now she understood the whole thing.

"We can leave Lace if you want", Melissa spoke empathically.

"No dear we are not leaving I came to have fun and I will, this is Wolfe's turf but I will have my fun tonight. He is well occupied", while adding more lipstick to my half painted lips.

On our way back to the table, a nice tall chocolate man approached me. He looked like Morris Chestnut, "Can I have this dance?" he asked politely.

"We'll of course you can", I said nicely.

When I looked over at Wolfe his eyes was on me. Morris and I two stepped it elegantly, he was handsome with a nice smile. I prayed for a slow song to play and it did, it brought Morris and I closer together.

The chick with Wolfe grabbed him to dance, and they joined the dance floor it was awkward I wanted to keep my eyes off of them. When she was so close to him I felt like I was on fire

I excused myself from Morris and I went to stand outside. Melissa didn't see me exit she was being entertained by another sexy man.

I stood outside to get my thoughts together. My mind was racing, I couldn't believe Wolfe or I couldn't believe myself. I made the decision and he has moved on in his life. I was crushed. I wanted to leave but then I would look defeated and I am not going to give my power away. I wanted him, I wanted to go upstairs and snatch him straight out that heffa's arms. And she is so damn pretty. My mind was racing.

It was a beautiful summer's night; the air was clear and crisp. I could have taken nice pictures of this scenery but I didn't have my camera on me.

"Small world" I heard his voice behind me. My heart thumbed.

"I guess", was all that would come out.

I turned to face him, "You look sexy, never seen you dressed up like this", he said looking straight at my legs.

Wolfe stood in a confident stance, he was strong his face resembled a Wolfe. That wasn't how he got his nick name from, it came from his father. He told me the story when he was a little boy all the kids followed him around the neighborhood wanting to be his friend. He was a natural leader his father told him all his life.

"You're like a Wolf always leading the pack son" his father would tell him and the name stuck from then.

"Thank you", I responded looking into his eyes.

"You may want to get back to your girlfriend", I snapped.

He took a deep breath and put his hands in his pocket. He was dressed to impress with black slacks on and short sleeve button down shirt that exposed his masculine built. The tattoo of the cross with his father's name showed, his hair was neatly cut and his cologne was nice, I checked him out from head to toe.

"You made the choice Lacy… you did", he said agitated.

"What the hell was I suppose to do Wolfe, my life was in disarray, I didn't want to hurt anyone else any further, that was hard for me", my eyes tearing up.

He just stared at me, "You're beautiful to me", he said.

I started to cry. I didn't want to do this with him right now, I wanted to fuck him right there on the steps. My heart was breaking.

"I can't do this", I started walking to my car. Wolfe didn't chase me or even call my name. I made it to my car and called Melissa. Her phone rang out to voicemail.

"Hey it's me, I'm in my car please, call me", I was crying.

Melissa called me back and made it to the car. She told me to go home and she understood the situation. She even offered to come home with me, I declined, and she wouldn't take no as an answer. I felt horrible spoiling her night like this. When Wolfe is involved it's never good. Melissa jumped in my car and said we will come back to get her car later.

Melissa was driving I was too upset. I couldn't believe he didn't even come to see if I was okay or not. He must have put his guards up and really put us to rest. I was angry with him, I was angry with myself. I wanted to scream but I stayed cool. We made a stop at Melissa's she needed to stop home to get something's; she was going to stay the night with me; with Bradley away and ShyAnn at Mrs. Krauss house, I really didn't want to be alone. It took her forever it seemed.

When we pulled up in my drive way a black SUV sat across the street. It looked like Wolfe's driver. I was half drunk and fully heartbroken with makeup that ran under my eyes. The back door opened to the black SUV.

"Lacey" he yelled

I turned and saw Wolfe standing in the middle of the street, "Come take a ride with me", he said.

I stood still.

"Now that's some Romeo shit right there and he fine as hell too Lace you better go with that man girl what you waiting for?".

"But I messed up your night already Mel, "

She cut me off, "Blah, blah, blah, listen I'm your best friend and I will always be your best friend but this is the man you love girl, go ahead I know how to get in your house and raid your fridge", She chuckled.

"Mel", I said feeling guilty.

"Go", she pointed her finger.

"I love you Mel", I said happily, and I turned and gave my best sexy strut to Wolfe.

*****

We ended up at one of the largest parks in the city that has beautiful waterfalls a black gate surrounded the falls, and two benches sat in front of it. The park had a sprinkle of people in it. It was late but the night was beautiful, I wish I had my camera. The car ride was silent; Wolfe just embraced me and held me tight.

As we stood in front of the falls we watched the water as if it had the magic potion to our confused hearts.

"I'm sorry Wolfe; I should not have given you the letter in that way… I was a coward".

"You shouldn't have given me the letter at all", Wolfe spoke plainly with his hands in his pockets.

I went to sit on one of the benches, and Wolfe sat down next to me, "When I was a little girl my mother was an alcoholic I didn't know this at the time because I was so young.

I remember going back and forth from place to place we lived out of 2 duffle bags. The longest we stayed in one place was maybe a year. She could never keep a job her demons was too big. As I became a teenager, I took small jobs wherever we were like packing groceries at stores or selling post cards I would get from a neighbor at one of our temporary locations. I was miserable.

She always told me to never call my father that he didn't care about us. A day after my fourteenth birthday my father found us at a friend's house. He told me to take my bag and took me from my mother. I didn't see my mother again until years later when she cleaned herself up. I promised myself that I would never allow that to happen to my daughter".

Tears were now in my eyes, and Wolfe moved closer to me. He wiped my tears away and said, "Let me meet her Lace".

I blinked twice surprised at his response. I looked back at the falls and stayed silent.

"I understand baby, I get it she is your baby and you want to protect her but let me meet her see how she reacts to my presence. Tell me what she loves to do and I will plan the day for us", Wolfe said.

I was thinking confused on how to reply. I wanted this to happen I loved this man clearly and he loved me, "I will consider that Wolfe, let me just think about it I don't want to make any decisions based on emotions right now but that I will consider".

Wolfe grabbed my hand we started walking toward little brick houses toward the back of the park, once we made it to the grassy part I took my heals off and Wolfe held them for me. We didn't see the falls at this time but we heard it clearly. The little brick house was bare with two benches, this part of the park was called lover's lane. Couples came to sit and talk, flirt, and make out it was beautiful scenery. It was deserted and inviting for Wolfe and me. I sat on the bench, Wolfe remained standing.

"I didn't know what I wanted in my life before I met you, when I first seen you I knew it was you that I was missing, I just knew from how I felt watching you do that shoot, I never was attracted to any woman in that way", Wolfe said.

I was looking at him calm but my heart was racing fast, Wolfe came and sat next to me I started rubbing his head, "I always said that I would never fall in love with a woman, not because I didn't want to but because I wasn't ready too. But I realize now that love has no time table when it comes you have to take it or you lose it. Do you love this man you lay next too at night?" he asked in a serious tone.

"I do love him, but I'm not in love with him", I said sadly.

"Do you want us?" he asked looking me in the eyes.

"I do" I spoke out loud.

"Then let's not waste no more time with this Lacey, let's do things the right way", Wolfe said.

I was all over the place with my emotions and didn't want to think about what was ahead dealing with Bradley. I knew that I was in love with Wolfe and wanted him. We started to kiss passionately, I got up and straddled him, and I pulled my dress up right above my ass to show my sexy black lace panties. I could feel the hardness of Wolfe's dick pushing up on his pants. He caressed my ass and rubbed my legs with aggression. I was licking his neck and sucking his earlobe, he loved that. His moans was arising me even more. My pussy was hot and wet.

I pulled his dick out and started to massage it gently, he moaned more. I continued to kiss him; I opened his shirt and started to give small pecks all over his chest still massaging his dick. I pushed my panties to the side and took all of him inside of me. I rotated my hips to a sexy rhythm. Wolfe was holding my tiny waist looking me in the eyes, which were turning me on even more.

My moans became louder over Wolfe's. This man was everything I wanted. We were fucking in the park, that was enough to bring me to my orgasm but Wolfe started to pump me from below, he moved me slightly to the left and hit my G spot. My orgasm was slow, the feeling was exhilarating I grabbed his back and held him tight Wolfe was coming too his body tightened up. We fixed each other up and sat on the bench of lover's lane embracing each other like we didn't want to let go.

"Can you come back with me to my place tonight?" Wolfe asked in a low tone.

I was surprised, I never been to his place before our escapades was always at fancy hotels, cars, the cabin but never his place, "As long as I'm home by 8, that's when I have to get Shy from my neighbor's house".

"Done", Wolfe said he grabbed my shoes, and my hand and walked back to his car, the driver saw us coming and got out to open the door for us.

Wolfe's house was beautiful, it was new and inviting. It looked like an interior decorator had something to do with it. His walls were snow white and his ceilings were high; he had nice pictures hanging and one wall had my three pictures I took and was paid nicely from the gallery the night I met him. Everything seemed new in his house, I couldn't believe he lived here alone. His living room wasn't as organized; it looked like someone actually lived here different than the kitchen and dining room. His bookshelf was filled with books that looked untouched, pictures of his family infested on top but neatly placed in order. I saw several pictures of him and his brother always smiling. The picture of his father and mother was beautiful. His parents made such a great couple, they looked happy and peaceful. Wolfe had pictures of each of his shops hanging in his hallway with the date each was opened. I was walking his house like a curious child.

"Make yourself comfortable Lace", Wolfe stated while making drinks behind his bar.

"Can I take a shower please?" I asked.

"You can do whatever you want to do baby, mi casa su casa, extra towels are in this closet and you can wear one of my t-shirts to sleep in".

"Or I can sleep with no shirt", I said smiling and winked at him.

Wolfe smiled at me and licked his lips.

Once I set the shower and lathered up I felt a cool breeze, Wolfe joined me in the shower we kissed and washed each other, we fucked again of course and then dried each other off and lotion each other down while in his California king bed, his bed was more comfortable than any bed I have ever been in, it was the same bed as in the cabin but seemed bigger. We sipped our drinks casually and talked about everything.

Wolfe explained to me about his worker Man-Man. I thought how special this must really be to do what he did for that young man. He filled me in that his brother will manage the Crestar shop in the village. I told him that I have been looking for property to open my own gallery. He was happy I made the decision and told me he was going to hook me up with some people that can help me with the process. He even offered to come with me to look. Wolfe was a man, he loved hard. He was a beast on the outside with his strong features and no non sense attitude but his heart was good. He paid attention to people. He thought about people's situations, and he wasn't so much a talker as he was a listener. I adored him, and I knew that I had to be with him.

We talked most of the night; he kissed my forehead before we fell asleep. My alarm came on and I wanted to throw it but I had to get Shy from Mrs. Krauss and talk to Melissa. I got up to use the bathroom and put on Wolfe's blue t-shirt that he had on. His scent still lingered in it, I went to the kitchen and made a quick omelet and toast for him. I was putting on my dress when Wolfe's phone starting ringing.

He picked it up in his sleepy voice, and then looked at the clock I sat in his chair and looked at him. His body was so thick and masculine, he was a beautiful man

"Good morning beautiful", Wolfe said.

96

"Hey sleepy head, I made you breakfast it's on the table".

"Thank you babe", Wolfe got up and went to the bathroom but kissed my cheek first.

When he got up his dick was hard as a rock, I wanted to fuck again but I knew if we did I would be late.

"My driver is outside waiting for you Lace", Wolfe said while in the bathroom.

I didn't want to leave but I knew I had to. Wolfe came over to me and hugged me I touched every ripple of his chiseled body and rubbed his back. Wolfe raised my chin to look in the eyes.

"Remember what we talked about, I want us keep in touch daily Lace let me know you ok call me when you can and I will do the same. Do what you got to do but time is of the essence. By the end of the week you have a date for me to set up our date with Shy, okay?"

"Okay", I said smiling at him.

"I love you girl", Wolfe said and hugged me tight.

His phone started to ring again, "That's the driver Lace, don't for get to keep in touch babe", Wolfe said.

"I will".

Wolfe walked me to the car and told the driver don't bother to get out, he got this. I smiled to myself. The drive home was emotional for me, I loved Wolfe if I messed this up then he will move on and I couldn't allow this to happen. But Bradley is going to be devastated, I had some hard decisions to make but my daughter was my priority.

I was feeling better about her meeting Wolfe than I did when he first proposed it yesterday. It made sense, she didn't have to know who he was she could just meet him and see how she reacts to him.

As far as Bradley I will have to think about how to go about this with him. I mean we have been so distant lately. He seems to want marriage for his family as if he has something to prove to them. By his sister getting married, I guess he feels pressured. But he doesn't express any love towards me at least the way I get it from Wolfe.

Is it fair to be with a man because they love my child like their own but lacks in loving me? I had a lot to think about, right now I just wanted to get ShyAnn and have a pow wow with Melissa. I shut myself away from Melissa after the letter to Wolfe. I just threw myself into my work and taking care of ShyAnn, I didn't want to continue to repeat my pain. Now I needed Melissa to hear my situation because if anyone is going to give it to me real, it will be her.

✳✳✳✳✳

I walked into my house at 7:00a.m. to find Melissa in the kitchen cooking breakfast it seemed for a family of 10. Bacon and sausage filled the air, when I texted her that I was on my way I didn't expect her to get up and be Betty Crocker but it sure did smell good.

"Look at Miss Thang right here, my quiet, nice, sweet organized best friend has her, own personal soap opera going on here; I'm jealous", Melissa laughed.

"Mel I need to talk to you and fast before I have to get Shy", I said quickly.

Mel had on a long t shirt pajama top and black scarf to hold her new weave in place, cute flip flops and a pretty face with no makeup.

"Well I'm all ears girlfriend what's the 411?" She said excitedly while placing my plate in front of me and a cup of coffee.

"Well damn, thanks girl I'm hungry as hell", I said.

"I'm sure you are that's what good sex does to us", she smirked.

I told Melissa the whole story from beginning to end. She kept smiling like my life wasn't at its wits end. This was my life I needed her to look past how sexy Wolfe was and focus on the whole scenario.

"Ok so now this delicious man told you that he is in love with you and wants to meet your daughter so that you can leave Bradley and start a new life with him?" She asked surprised.

I shifted in my seat, "Yeah Mel that's about right...I'm so confused".

"Ok seriously Lace let's look at it like this, you know something is up with Bradley I mean you barely have sex with him, he shows you no affection, and your holding on for Shy's sake. I mean I get that part but Bradley isn't your husband yet, if you're going to make a move make it now that it's no ties".

"I know but ShyAnn".

Melissa cut me off, "ShyAnn will be fine Lace, she's a smart girl. You are not your mother Lacey, you are better than that. This man may be it for you; he makes you happy; he's protective, he's involved in your career or maybe he's not it for you but you will never know; all we know is that he's more of everything than Bradley now except for ShyAnn's sake but that too can change. I mean he has your work hanging in his house. Now, can he be a total fuck up in a year or two? Most men are but if he's who he say he is then this may be what you need to make you happy, I mean what man is looking to take on someone else's kid in this way?"

I looked at Melissa and took a deep breath

"I mean look at it like this do things in slow motion, don't rush anything Lace. Let him meet Shy see how that goes you have to make decisions as time goes on. Have a plan for sure; take a chance girl sometimes you can't stay in your safe zone forever. And you have money Lacey, you can take care of you and Shy with no worries if this thing with Wolfe fails", Melissa spoke serious this time.

"What about Bradley's feelings?" I asked like a lost child.

"Bradley is a grown man Lace. He will be fine I mean someone is going to get hurt in this situation better him then you. Don't get me wrong I applaud him for stepping in with Shy you were a mess when her dad was murdered. That is to never be forgotten but, you are a beautiful woman that deserves to feel love and if he can't supply that then you have to let that go".

"My grandmother use to say, 'whomever we wasn't born with, we can learn to live without them', I said after thinking to myself. Mel winked at me.

"What your saying is right Mel, I just have to be cautious is all I mean it hasn't been a year yet since I've known Wolfe besides on the level of romance and sex. I see what he does for me, how he looks at me, I mean I adore him but passion for a man, and a man being a father figure to my daughter is two different things".

Mel took a sip of her coffee, "You are not going to know anything if you don't try Lace. Listen to me let her meet Wolfe; you say he has a cabin upstate, take her there out the ordinary. Tell Bradley we are all going as a girls vacation or something for the weekend, anything. And speak to Shy Ann tell her something that will make sense to a 6 year old. Let that be your first step, if she likes him great if not then you have to decide what's next but you have to start doing something".

"Your right, I will do the cabin idea it will give me ample time, and I can think clearer up there she may seem a little confused at first but she will be fine". I convinced myself.

"Now you're talking girlfriend, and remember this Lace life is short this man isn't going to wait around forever, I mean he's fine as hell and well to do. Women must flock at him daily, and he wants you, you can't fuck that up, and what's up with the china doll he was with?" Melissa snapped.

"He said she is a manager at one of his shops and a good friend that he has sex with time from time. She goes out with him and he cares for her but he doesn't love her", I said pushing up my shoulders.

"I guess that's fair, I mean he was honest", Melissa said.

"Yeah he was and what can I say, I have my situation here he owes me no loyalty at this point", I said sadly.

"Oh but that must burn you up to know that china doll gets all that sexiness", Melissa teased.

"Not funny Mel, not funny at all but truth is she can have his body, I have his heart and that's all that matters to me", I rolled my eyes.

"I know that's right", Melissa cracked up laughing.

I called Mrs. Krauss and asked could she bring ShyAnn home I wanted to take another shower and put some comfortable clothes on.

Melissa said she would stay until Bradley came home. She is Shy Ann's Godmother so she wanted to spend some time with her. Shy Ann loves Melissa so when she came home she was excited to see her.

I texted Wolfe to tell him that everything was okay, and the plan to take Shy Ann to the cabin. I just had to make a date for a weekend coming up so I had to move my schedule around and think of a great lie for Bradley. While Shy and Mel was downstairs playing dolls I went into my bedroom to straighten some things up.

When I was fixing up Bradley's clothes in his closet I saw a box underneath his brown hard bottoms. I became curious, I'm not a snoop but something was making me want to know why this box was almost hidden. I opened and seen loose ties, some credit card bills stamped "paid in full "and a white envelope with no name on it. I opened it and started to read it.

Bradley,

I hope this letter finds you well; I can't stop thinking about you. Our last time together in Vegas was unforgettable. I hate to have us this way; I hate the secrecy and hidden agendas. I know no one will understand us, it's difficult to live this lie this way but in time I believe we will be together. Writing this letter is easier than sending an email, it reminds me back in the days when words really meant something. I really wanted to be at your sister's wedding but my schedule won't allow it please forgive me. I will make this up to you. I don't want to run on too long just know that I love you and can't wait to lie in your arms again lover.

Tracy

I sat with the letter in my hands and didn't know how to feel. How old was this letter? It's no address, no date which means did he take it from the original envelope and place in this one? It also disturbs me that he invited this chick to his wedding, I mean the audacity of him. The distance makes since now. Tracy? I didn't know if I should be happy about this or sad. We both were in love with someone else. We both were living secret lives.

This made my decision so much easier. I couldn't tell anyone anything right now, I had to investigate and see what this was so when it all comes out I'm in a stronger position. Part of me felt betrayed, but I knew that I couldn't dare feel this way when I myself have been unfaithful. Bradley went to Vegas a couple of months ago, a month right before Wolfe and I went to the cabin for the first time. And he went last year also; he said it was a convention. I guess we are both liars, and sneaks. We find ways to escape us.

I have been so caught up with Wolfe that I haven't really noticed anything besides our distance and his unaffectionate ways. I didn't know how to feel, I wanted to feel bad but I couldn't. This put me a great position but made me feel so ignorant. What if I didn't have Wolfe? I can't tell Melissa about this right now, she'll put batteries in my back. I have to think about this and put myself in a good position.

The one thing I was clear about was that ShyAnn was going to meet Wolfe and that was clear. I was going to leave Bradley anyway this just gave me a greater reason. If this person loves him so, and he loves her then he should be with her. I convinced myself that this was the best thing that could have happened.

When Bradley comes home tonight I will act like I always do—desperate for attention. It depends on how he's going to come home, he might be all over me or he might be distant. I'm sure he was with her on this overnight stay.

The house phone was ringing; I rushed and placed all his stuff back nice and neat just the way I found it. I put the envelope back but I took the letter, I needed it when the right time came.

"Mommy, mommy, it's Brad-Brad on the phone" ShyAnn ran into the room and handed me the phone.

"Hey", was all I could think of, "Hey Lacy how is everything?"

"It's going ok Bradley and you, How's the trip?"

"It's ok, I'm going to have to stay another day due to paper work mix up from one of the other competitors", he said.

"Oh, ok well when do you think you will be home?" I asked happy that I had time to think more about this.

"No later than Tuesday, I will call you when I get to the airport", he sounded in a rush.

"Ok, not a problem" I said.

When we hung up I sat on my bed with the phone still in my hands, and thought about life for me now and life for what's to come. I can really have Wolfe and he can have me the way we want it. That was enough for me to jump up and down but I wasn't feeling that excited. I needed to think, I am a good thinker as long as I'm not in my feelings.

I called Wolfe and he was surprised about my call, I told him that I wanted to see him tomorrow he didn't hesitate. He told me to come to his house; he will clear his schedule and have Karen do the business. I felt special; he was a businessman to heart but would put it all aside for me. I just wanted to be in his arms. I wasn't going to tell Wolfe about Bradley's lover, I didn't want him to rush this any faster. This was my true secret no one knew I knew but the good Lord and that was the way I was going to keep it. Karen, that was the lady I seen at the party at the hotel, I knew I seen her before. I was never introduced to her personally just remember talking to Wolfe about her and he mentioned she was at the gallery that night. Karen is his best friend and business partner; she's gay but fierce and beautiful.

I told Melissa to get dress I was taking us out for dinner tonight, it was my treat. She was down for it and Shy Ann was excited. I told them that Bradley would be home Tuesday instead of tonight and I didn't feel like cooking.

Melissa and I made arrangements to pick up her car from the hotel where the party was, and then we can go out to celebrate. Well at least it my own private celebration. I was able to have the man that I love without the guilt to follow me or would it still exist in me? I knew that I had no right to feel this good about something so bad, but I couldn't help my feelings. Life was turning out to be more unexpected than I thought.

Once we finished dinner Shy Ann and I said our goodbye's to Melissa and came home to have mommy daughter time. I wanted to talk to Shy Ann about something's just to try and prepare her for something's. After she took her bath and put her pajamas on, I read her, her favorite bedtime story and sat in her bed with her.

"ShyAnn I know you love Brad-Brad very much", I said.

"Yes I do mommy he is the best man ever", she chimed.

"You know things change in life and if mommy and Brad-Brad had to separate for whatever reason, how would you feel?"

She was quiet for a moment, "You mean separate forever?"

"Well not forever, you may still see him but maybe not everyday".

"Oh, I will miss him very much mommy", she said.

I was quiet, I rubbed her hair gently, "Are we going somewhere mommy?" she asked.

"Not now sweet pea but in time we may I just want you to be okay".

"As long as I am with you, mommy, I will be okay".

I smiled and kissed her, "Ok now it's time to say your prayers, you have one week of school left and early morning rising", I shook her in a playful way.

ShyAnn got on her knees and folded her hands.

"Now I lay me down to sleep I pray my soul for God to keep, if I should die before I wake I pray my soul for God to take,

God bless my mommy, Brad-Brad, auntie Mel, Mrs. Krauss, all the good people and all the bad people in the world, and God please help my mommy be strong with or without Brad-Brad in the name of Jesus Amen".

"Amen" I said

My eyes widened and tears started to fall from my eyes.

I got myself together and tucked her in tight, "Have mommy ever told you how smart you are sweet pea?"

"All the time mommy", she smiled.

"I love you baby".

I left my child's room feeling elated. Shy would be just fine just like Melissa said. Maybe I was really allowing the dysfunction of my childhood cloud the good job as a mom that I was providing for Shy. I wanted her to have it safe and loving and with Wolfe it must be the same. Wolfe loves me, so I know he will love ShyAnn.

Bradley started off loving me now time has allowed things and feelings to change. I never felt with Bradley what I feel with Wolfe, it's just something about him that's so different. I felt good about our future. And the truth is, if Wolfe changes like Bradley has then I will not make the same mistake twice. I must learn to love myself to know that I deserve the best for me because it's then that I can give the best to ShyAnn, when I'm happy she's happy. When I'm okay she's okay. I fell asleep thinking about my day with Wolfe, it's nothing like having something great to look forward too.

WOLFE

APPRECIATION

I had the cleaning lady come by 6:00a.m. I heard her moving around when I opened my eyes. I wanted the place to be in tip top shape when Lacy arrived. I was surprised that she called me and said she wanted to see me. I was use to months going by before I saw her. I also have Mrs. Wilson my neighbor coming over she's going to cook Lacy and I a southern brunch. This woman is the best cook I would never tell my mom's that though but she's good. She's retired and can always use the extra money. I give her more than she charges because next to mom she's the sweetest woman I know. I donate to her church and fund any charities they do, she really doesn't like to take money from me but I told her that she's worth every cent. And she will take it and tuck it in her bra.

I got up and did some sit ups, and pull ups on my pull up bar. I did push up until the sweat started to pour down my face. I wanted my body to be tight for Lace. As I was preparing for my shower my phone rang it was Man-Man.

"Talk to me".

"Wolfe what's up? Sorry to bother you so early I wanted to know if you can meet me at the shop later". Man-Man said.

"What's up is everything ok?" I asked.

"Yeah it's all good, I just did something's and wanted to run it past you face to face is all", Man-Man said calmly.

"Ok but it has be later I have plans for the morning".

"That's cool; you think you can get there before 4:00p.m.?"

"Not sure but I will hit you up in a text when I'm in route", I said. "You sure it's nothing you want to tell me now?"

"Nah Wolfe, it's all good just trying to be the man you teaching me to be real responsible is all", he sounded proud.

"Ok then Man, make that money, I'll holla".

"Peace".

I chuckled at this kid, he was on point. He just needed someone to believe in him. My father told me very young 'give a man a fish he'll eat for a day, teach him how to fish and he'll eat for a lifetime'. I'm glad I was able to teach him how to fish.

Lacy was coming by as soon as she dropped off her daughter at school, I estimated 8:45a.m... I called Mrs. Wilson she was there in 15 minutes with her grandson in tow he was carrying bags for her. Mrs. Wilson's round statue made her seem intimidating but her plump round face made her look likes aunt jemima. I was grateful for my southern neighbor; Lacy only gets the very best. I could have taken her to an expensive place to wine and dine her but the small things counts with Lacy; she'll appreciate this much more. Mrs. Wilson moved around the kitchen like a professional.

"I shoo do like cooking in your kitchen Wolfe, it's like being on T.V.", she chuckled.

"Mi casa su casa Mrs.W; anytime!"

"You sure is handsome she came and pinched my cheek, I know why the ladies be all over you and you the nicest young man I ever known, giving, and loyal just like your daddy".

I was looking at Mrs. Wilson but thinking about my pops, he was a hell of a man. Mrs. Wilson knows my whole family; her sons always went to my pops shop to get their haircuts. Once Mrs. Wilson's husband died she used the insurance money to buy her the house next to mine and let her daughters and three granddaughters move in with her.

"Thank you young lady", I said to her before excusing myself.

My cleaning lady did a good job, everything was on point. I didn't bother dressing up this go around I kept my basketball shorts on, with socks and my black wife beater. Once Mrs. Wilson leaves I have Lacy here by myself we just going to cuddle and make love all day. I wondered where the hell her man is at that she has time to come and check me. But that didn't matter as long as she was here is all I cared about. White girl just shot me text message, she wants to see me. I ignored it.

The doorbell rang, and fried fish was in the air. It was Lacy; she was sexy as hell today. I have to get use to seeing her like this. I mean she's beautiful regardless with sweats and sneakers but baby got on some tight blue jeans that show her round hips and a low cut blouse and black pumps. I licked my lips.

"How can I help you?" I joked. She hugged me, she smelled good I didn't want to let her go, "You look good girl, turn around let daddy see you", I joked again.

"Stop it silly", her lips looked perfect.

"It smells good in here Wolfe, you cooking", she asked.

"Yeah, all for you, baby girl", I walked behind her with my arms in front of her. Mrs. Wilson was focused, and lit up when she saw Lacy.

"Well hello beautiful" Mrs. Wilson said.

"I would shake your hand but I got this cornmeal on my hands", she laughed.

"Lacy this is my neighbor the beautiful Mrs. Wilson, Mrs. Wilson this is Lacy Grant my lady", I said proudly.

"Your lady, well that's new to hear. You must be a real special lady if I'm in here cooking for yah. Wolfe is one fine man, you're a lucky woman".

"Nice to meet you", Lacy said with a broad smile. "It smells wonderful in here".

"Well thank you baby", said Mrs. Wilson with a big smile.

"It tastes as good as it smells", I stated.

Lacy and I left Mrs. Wilson to finish off her perfection, we sat on the couch I couldn't stop staring at her, "I'm surprised you called me" I said to her moving lint from her eye lash.

Lacy started kissing me all tongue; she was sucking my bottom lip, rubbing my arms. Something was up with her she seemed more relaxed, happier.

"I like this Lacy, what's up with you girl?" I said holding her face.

"What, I can't kiss my man?" She said like a real black girl rolling her eyes.

I looked and seen that her engagement was off her hand replaced by a nice black custom ring, "Something happened you want to tell me about it?" I asked her curiously.

"Nope, just wanted to be here with you", she said confidently.

The scent of food in the air was making me more and more hungry.

"You had Mrs. Wilson come and cook for us?" She asked.

"Hell yeah, you have to taste her cooking I promise you'll be begging for more".

Just then Mrs. Wilson called us to eat; the table was set up like a feast. She cooked fried fish, salmon cakes, and grits with butter, scrambled eggs, homemade biscuits, turkey bacon and fresh orange juice, with a pot of coffee. Lacey's eyes couldn't believe it. "My goodness Mrs. Wilson this looks delicious, Wolfe you trying to make me fat". Lacey said smiling

"Ain't nothing like a good meal child, and you can spare some meat with that tiny waist of yours", Mrs. Wilson chuckled.

"Only the best for you Lace, only the best", I said as I sat down.

"Well I'm going to leave you lovebirds to feast, please enjoy". Mrs. Wilson started gathering up her things and humming that sound like a church song I remember growing up as a kid.

"Wolfe don't worry about this one, this was for you and your special lady", Mrs. Wilson winked at me.

I just smiled at her, because I already put cash in an envelope and stuck it in her bag when she wasn't looking.

Lacey and I ate like a king and queen; it was different with her this time. She smiled more and was cracking jokes that actually made me laugh. I looked at her with lust and love. She was so beautiful to me.

"I want you to stay the night with me tonight", I said to her in between chuckles.

"Wolfe I can't, I want to baby but I can't he will be home tomorrow and I want to be there as normal as I can plus ShyAnn is in her last week of school".

I took a deep breath and understood her situation, "But I will call and have Melissa pick Shy up from school, and leave around midnight", she negotiated.

"That's cool babe, I just want to be with you is all", I said then wiped something from her lip.

"I have to go to one of the shops later, I want you to roll with me but that's late afternoon right now I just want to lick you like a lollipop".

Lacey smiled that winning smiling at me, and then engaged the sexy look; we finished up our food and went to the living room. Lacey took off her pretty pumps and laid her head on my lap, I played with her hair it looked like she just got it done.

"You were right Wolfe that was the best food I have ever eaten, Mrs. Wilson knows her shit in the kitchen, I'm so stuffed that's an extra hour of cardio a day for me for like two weeks", she said and rubbed her stomach.

"Cut it out baby girl, all you need is me I'm that treadmill and bike", I told her kissing her forehead.

We were full from the meal, I didn't want to rush sex I wanted to enjoy my lady because I know that sex was going to come eventually and I wanted it bad too. But we had something's to discuss like meeting with her daughter and how this was going to happen. Lacy had it all planned. I was surprised she had it all laid out. Something changed in her world, I want to stroke my ego and believe it was me but at the same time I didn't really know. I thought maybe she seeing me with China changed her mind. At this point it really didn't matter we were getting closer to being with one another exclusively so I was going to just enjoy the moment.

119

My phone was ringing and brought both of us out of our niggaitis good food will do that to you.

'"Speak to me", I said groggy.

"Hey partner its K, can you talk?"

"Holler at me K, what's good out there?"

Karen spoke to me about the business of the shops, she closed a lot of loopholes and I was grateful for that. I got up and laid Lacey's head gently on a pillow on the couch. She didn't wake up.

I told Karen that Man-Man wanted to see me at the shop and asked her did she know about anything that was going on there. She told me that she didn't know so it must not have been anything for me to concern myself about. But she assured me that I should show up there just in case.

I was going for sure but I wanted to eat Lacey like some pink starburst first. After hanging up with Karen I always felt good, she was so on point with the business.

I went back to couch and started kissing Lacy on the neck; it was one of her weak spots. She started to moan, I started to undress her, and the smell of her body was a fresh cotton scent. It made me want her even more. When I took her pants down she had on blue lace Victoria secret panties, he panties and bra's was always so sexy. Lacy started waking up.

"Wolfe baby", she groaned out of her sleep.

"Shhhhh, let me enjoy you, baby-girl".

I opened her legs after removing her pretty panties and started kissing her inner thigh, her legs are so pretty, I gently bit her inner thigh she arched her back slightly.

Her pussy smelled like cotton fresh, she was freshly shaven and I opened her lips and started sucking on her clitoris nice and slow, she was moaning louder, it was weak spot I learned her weak spots for sex, sucking her clitoris gently was one of them.

I started licking of vulva walls always ending that lick at her clitoris, she was crying in moans by this time. She grabbed my head and started crying my name, I licked and sucked all her juices, I stuck two fingers inside her hot pussy, and she was wetter than a water fountain.

My dick was hard and I was ready to feel her inside of me. I wanted her bad-her crying moans and thick legs around my back and the smell and taste of her was driving me crazy. Lacy loves to be in control while we make love but today I will control this.

Lacy came all in my mouth, her juices tasted good, I went back to her mouth and kiss her deep she was licking her juices off of my lips. That turned me on even more.

We made it to the bed and I entered her while she was on her back and her legs were up in the air. Her eyes was so beautiful, I loved the fact that this woman was so damn sexual. She made the sexiest love faces and her cries of pleasure were better than any music I ever heard. I stroked her deeply and felt her insides.

"I love you baby girl", I whispered in her ear as I was pumping gently.

"I love you too Wolfe", she seductively spoke in between moans.

After more strokes and rhythms in and out of her pussy, she told me she was going to cum again, I couldn't hold out anymore I needed to bust. I was all ready to cum inside the condom inside of her but she pushed me up snatched off the condom and sucked my dick until I came in her mouth and she swallowed it. I was speechless.

It felt so damn good and I was caught off guard which made it even better. She then grabbed my head and made me kiss her tongue and all. If you asked me, I would have done that yesterday, I would have said hell no. But this woman was something else. I mean she's absolutely sexually spontaneous. I can't lose her; I can't imagine her giving this good pussy to no other man. And the faster she gets out of that situation the better it's going to be for us. I was fucking chicks here and there but it stung me to think that Negro she lay next too gets all of this good loving. But I know that was her situation and I can't get all in my feelings about that. I wasn't stopping until Lacy was ALL mines.

We took a hot shower together and had sex again, this time she wanted me to fuck her in her ass from the beginning, and I couldn't control my appetite with this woman.

Nothing was ever the same with her, she was giving me her all no doubt. I never know what to expect from the quiet woman that loves taking pictures and holds all her beauty on another level. Lacy was a straight freak and I was happy as hell to have her, I couldn't let her know how much I truly loved her but I do more than I have loved any woman in my life. I just couldn't lose her again no matter what.

It started to rain outside, I opened the window it was something about the sound of rain that relaxes me- she feels the same. We fell asleep until my alarm woke us up at 3:00p.m.

"Lace let's get dress I want to take you with me to the new shop so you can see it and meet my new manager Man-Man, then we can go out to eat".

"How about I cook for you tonight instead of us going out?"she asked excited.

I looked at her and something in me jumped, this woman was going to be my wife no doubt, "Ok, that's cool, I know you can throw some breakfast together, but a dinner", I looked at her surprised.

"Well I'm no Mrs. Wilson but I come from roots that cooking is what did to celebrate every occasion", she spoke proudly.

"Well okay then it's settled then Lacy Grant is going to cook for me tonight", I stated like an announcement.

We got dressed and I decided to drive my Range instead of having my driver, I wanted to be in control. I wanted Lacy to ride shot gun with me today. I felt complete with her. Her pretty brown eyes are enough to make me weak but she has so much more to offer and I can't lose that.

When we got to the shop is was quiet, Frank is an older man that just comes and sits around the shop. He is a retired Veteran they tell me. No one minds his presence, he's innocent he will sweep up some hair, or wipe down some mirrors and I told Man-Man to give him something every now and then. Man Man said sometimes he takes it, and sometimes he doesn't. When we walked in no one was around.

"Frank, what's good…this here this is my lady Lacy…
Lacy this is Frank he helps out around the shop".

Frank stood and saluted Lacy like he would have in the
army, she smiled and he smiled back, "Nice to meet you Frank",
Lacy said.

"Yo, where the hell is everybody at Frank? Man-Man, the
other barbers?"

"Oh they all in the back eating", he said it quickly.

"Eating? All of them at the same time?" I said pissed off,
sort of.

I was confused and shit, my shop is empty which is whack
and then these Negros are eating like it's all good. I'm going to
have to talk to Man-Man and Pete about this shit. I grabbed
Lacy's hand and we started walking towards the back of the shop,
when I opened the door it was dark, and then lights popped on
and the room was filled with mad people, food and big ass cake in
the middle.

"Surprise!" they all screamed.

"Oh shit", I said and let Lacy hand go.

"Wow", I heard Lacy say.

Man-Man approached me and gave me hug and a pound.

125

"What's this?" I asked happy, surprised and confused all at the same damn time.

"Just have a seat right here boss, and you'll see".

I was still shocked; Karen came up to me and hugged me. I looked at her and smirked, Kem was there he came and gave me a hug; my mom was there, some faces I knew some I didn't know. Sash and Pete was there I was shocked. Lacy was smiling from ear to ear she looked just as confused and surprised as I did so I knew that she didn't know.

I sat down told Man-Man to get a chair for Lacy, he brought a folded chair I whispered and told him to get my lady a better chair than that. He brought her back my comfortable chair from my office.

Man-Man's girl and baby was there, people from the community board was there and was presenting me with an award for helping the community. They appreciated the fact that we hired some people from the neighborhood, and we discounted our prices for the students and elderly. They awarded me with a black business owner award. I was surprised, I mean I have one from my uptown shop but this was quick.

Once the community leaders finished they told me to hold off coming up there to get the award because Man-Man had something to say, Man-Man said words about me that night that I will never forget. He started tearing up in front of everyone, when he was finished it wasn't one dry eye. I didn't cry but I was touched. Lacy's eyes wouldn't stop crying; I held her hand and squeezed it. Karen came and sat on the other side of me. To my surprise Man-Man's girl went up to the mic after him with a beautiful arrangement of synthetic roses that was my favorite color burgundy and blue with white. The back of the roses had a plate that read 'changing one life at a time'. It was beautiful.

Once it was my time to go up, I was speechless but I knew I had to say something. I went and said my thank you and showed my appreciation. Hugs came from everyone. Before it ended Karen stood at the mic and announced that our barbershops were the leading small business in sales in all five Boro's. She spoke on how efficient and hardworking all the employee's have been and then thanked everyone for coming out and supporting us.

After the applause, it was an enormous board of food that filled two tables with plenty of drinks and desserts. "Hey you, you were surprised?" Karen said laughing at me.

"Real slick K, real slick but it's all good, I can't believe y'all pulled this together you know a lot can't get passed me but y'all got me on this one", Karen looked at Lacy, then back at me- I looked at Karen to say to her, we'll talk later

"Lacy Grant, this is my partner and good friend Karen Bloomfield", I introduced and Lacy stood up to shake Karen's hand.

"Nice to finally meet you", Lacy said with a smile.

"Yes, I've heard a lot about you", Karen said in an indignant way.

Lacy looked at Karen strangely, "I'm going to introduce Lacy to my mother that is eyeing me in the corner and everyone else" I said and grabbed Lacy's hand.

My mother loved Lacy immediately; I didn't tell my mother the whole story about Lacy. She was so used to me having one female after the other I never bothered telling her my truth. But I knew my mom saw something different in Lacy.

I left Lacy with my mother and made my rounds to everyone who came out. The local newspaper was there; they wanted to make this front page for tomorrow so I took some pictures and gave my caption. I then went to Man-Man and his girl and told them how much I appreciate them acknowledging me.

I told his girl how beautiful the roses were; she told me that she made them herself. It was a hobby of hers and she did this especially for me. She was a sweet girl that southern drool and innocent look on her face made me think of how lucky Man-Man was. He had a beautiful baby and a good girl. As much as I had, I didn't have what he had. But I knew it was in time so I embraced this young family.

I then spoke with Pete and Sash and they assured me that the other shops were functioning well. They had all aspects covered. Karen came over; she told me that the soul food place and Chinese restaurant donated all the food we had here. The bakery down the block did all of the desserts and cake and the bodega gave some of the drinks which means nothing came from the shop or anyone's pocket. I was impressed.

I knew Karen was great with her business and worked that shit well. I was proud to have these good people around me. I looked and saw Lacy laughing with my mom, both of them was looking at me. I smiled.

"So, camera girl came back?" Karen asked curiously.

"You said if she comes back, she's mine", I said in my defense.

"Yes, I did but you better be sure this time it's for good, I just don't want you hurting Wolfe", she said and I saw the sincerity in Karen's eyes.

"China was going to come by the shop, but she had more work then she expected, what would you have done then?" She asked.

"Just what I'm doing now, China knows about Lacy…she knows there is no comparison. She doesn't like it but she knows I'm going to do what I'm going to do", I said confidently.

"As long as you feel like you got this, then I'm good", Karen said.

"K be nice to her, for real she's a good woman", I said in a serious tone, Karen looked at me in defeat.

"And let the record show, I'm a grown man; I can handle whatever comes to me. I made my choices", I looked at Karen with assurance.

"Yeah Mr. Drink himself into a stupor man", she joked.

"Your funny", I replied.

"Just know I'm here Wolfe, regardless-I got you". She added seriously.

"I know you do", I hugged Karen.

I made rounds and spoke to my brother for a minute, he and I was getting up tomorrow to talk business and bullshit. He keeps telling me that I should let him move in with me because I have so much room. I told that chump that I have that space for my family one day. He just laughed at me. We brought Kem a condo uptown a month before his release; it's a nice two bedroom in a great neighborhood. I spoke to my mom she told me that I had to invite Lacy over for dinner and looked at me like she knew something that I didn't. I gave her a kiss and told Kem to make sure mom got home safe.

Lacy and I didn't eat; I was waiting for my home cooked food she was going to cook for me. We took cake with us. Once we said our goodbyes we left for them to enjoy. Man-Man put my roses and plague in the back of my Range and we agreed that we will meet to talk business tomorrow.

Before I pulled off, Lacy reached over and kissed me deep. She sucked my bottom lip and squeezed my nose, "I'm so damn proud of you baby, really I am", Lacy said in a serious tone.

"Thanks baby girl"

"You are one special man, and I know that for fact", Lacy said.

I smiled and kissed her forehead. I was feeling good, I didn't expect Lacy to see this part of me but I guess it was meant to be.

We stopped at the supermarket and Lacy brought all the things she needed for dinner. At the checkout I pulled out my money and Lacy wanted to pay. I guess the look on my face she backed off.

No woman I ever dealt with wanted to pay for anything and this woman will pay and give without question. But she had to understand that I am here to take care of her, and she will never pay for anything as long as I'm around, even when I'm not around I will give her one of my cards with a nice limit that she can use. She doesn't know that but once we're exclusive that's my plans.

We got to the house and were getting out of the car when I spotted China sitting in her car in the front of the house. At first Lacy didn't see her but then she did. I was cool, China knew what time it was but I was curious to why she sat waiting for me. I brought all the bags in the house placed them on the table it was silence between us.

"I didn't know she was coming here", I said in my defense.

"No worries, I still have my situation- go handle your business I will start cooking", Lacy said without looking at me. I didn't know what to think.

I grabbed her and looked her in eyes, "She means nothing to me baby girl you understand, nothing! And she knows this but its business too with her so I will set it straight with her tonight so she will know for sure".

Lacy was silent.

"Lace, say something I don't want our night ruined by this", I pleaded.

"Handle your business Wolfe, I'm here", she said plainly.

I went outside and got in China's car. It smelled like fresh Vanilla, she was looking at me and I was looking straight, "Why are you here?" I asked her.

"I wanted to see you and congratulate you for your award tonight", she said.

"You could have sent a text message China", I said dryly.

"I could of but I didn't", she said with an attitude.

I took a deep breath and watched and Asian dog shake side to side that was pasted on her dashboard, "You know how I'm feeling about her".

"Yeah I know, but she is still attached and I'm not. I care for you, you know this", she whined.

"I know but we were never a couple, we had an understanding you know about the others why you tripping about Lacy?"

"She is a threat to us, I feel like I'm losing you completely", she stated.

I closed my eyes and felt a headache coming along, "China, look you're a great business woman you have been loyal to me and I care about you for that. We did our thing, and it's all good when we are together but no more Ma, I want to be with her".

China started crying, "Come on China don't do this now, for real", I was agitated.

"Wow Wolfe it's that easy for you, you can just cut on a cut off just like that well I can't. It's not right that you can do this without thinking about no one but yourself", she was pissed.

"China she is who I'm going to be with, I'm sorry if I hurt you in anyway but I was real with you from day one. We were cool and we had benefits to our friendship. I gave you the best of everything when we met up, the finest restaurants, I took you shopping even this car your driving don't act like I didn't."

"Your right, but didn't our friendship mean anything to you at all?" China pleaded.

"Of course and we will always be cool no doubt about that", I reached into my pocket and took out tissue and passed it her, she wouldn't take it. I put it on the dashboard. She had slow songs coming out of her speakers on low.

"Listen, you're doing well at the shop, Karen said your books are on point as usual, you're a beautiful girl, and life goes on".

She sat silent for a moment, then said, "I want to talk to her".

"No. For what, you have no dealing with her. Not now anyway keep away", I said angrily.

"I want to look in her eyes and see what she has that I don't have", she said sadly.

"China you're not going near her I promise you that, I'm sorry your hurting girl I am and I didn't ask for this. But you knew we was what we was it was no promises."

She went for her radio, and started playing "Foolish by Ashanti". I listened but I wanted to get out the car. The song was talking to me. I felt Ashanti's pain as I did China's.

Once the song was over I asked China "Is that it?"

"Fuck you Wolfe", she spat.

"Look your bitter if this is going to fuck up the shop let me know now, I care for you but my businesses are important if you can't handle it let me know I don't want this to go sour".

She laughed at me, "Look, I'm good I will never do that but by winter I will be looking to move on", she said.

I thought about that for a minute, "Don't fuck me over China, you're a grown woman Karen can take over for now if you in your feelings".

"Look at you, so easy to replace me, with business and personal. Wow, I am a fucking fool", she hissed.

"Life happens to us everyday China, my intentions weren't to hurt you at all-I'm here for you as a friend, you need me holla". She remained silent again, I leaned over and kissed her cheek and got out of the car.

She peeled off and I was concerned about her. She had keys to my shop and all the books. I called Karen told her the situation, and told her I needed her to take care of this for me. Keep an eye out on the shop and the books needed to be checked daily. First short China got to go. She agreed and told me that's why I shouldn't shit where I lay but I ignored that. I knew better. Lacy wasn't invited into my life she showed up like a gifted tornado. I stood outside my door; I smelled her food cooking it brought some peace to me. I just have to talk to Lacy real tonight.

I want her, and I want us to understand each other on truth. I will fight for her, whatever I had to do but losing her again isn't an option. Street codes are out the window with her, she's getting my all.

Lacy was sitting at the dining room table looking through her phone. I took her phone and placed it down on the table gently. I grabbed both of hands to stand her up; I hugged her tight and kissed her neck. She remained silent.

"Smells good baby girl"

She looked at me with those pretty brown eyes, "Is this going to be messy?" She asked ignoring my compliment.

"Right now no, I did what I had to do. I told her that it's all about you period".

"And she just said "Ok" and left", she snapped.

"No, she's bitter and hurt and I apologized for that, but I was clear that we had what we had and it's no more", I said.

Lacy let it go and went to look at the food in silence.

"Look Lace we need to talk about this, I'm not going to lose you over this bullshit. I need us to be on the same page. You still lay with that man at night".

She stopped and looked at me, "Your right Wolfe that's why I have nothing I can say, I'm defenseless, I get that. And that is what feels so bad". She was pissed.

"All you need to know is that I want you...period, I have to clean up some shit with some chicks and I will one at a time but you have loops to close too and I'm going to be patient and wait on that because I love you". She came to me and hugged me tight

When dinner was ready she served me like a king. She brought my plate to me like my mother use to do to my father. It made me feel more in love with her. She wanted to take care of me. The food was good; I ate every ounce on my plate. We went into the living room after making drinks it was 10:00p.m. this only gave a couple of more hours to be together before she had to leave. Those thoughts hurt me but I had to be patient. I had to understand her situation. She would be lying in bed with her dude and I will be in mine empty thinking of her. My insides were on fire.

Lacy rode me like a champion that night, she fucked me like never before. She was beautiful to me. After we fucked, we lay in each other's arms and talked. She told me she was prepared to leave her situation. She told me that once I met her daughter that it wouldn't be long before she was out. But she said she did have business to take care of in the process, she couldn't just walk away she had to protect certain assets. I knew what she meant.

She assured me that her heart belonged to me and that we will be together as much as possible until it was final. She spoke so assured to me tonight that it calmed that fire in me. She told me that she will be thinking about me when she's lying next to him and that they haven't had sex in weeks. That made me feel better but I couldn't believe some parts of it although I wanted to.

We talked about my mom and how much she adored her. She was ready to start a new chapter in her life. I told her why I started hustling when I was younger, my father and I had a big blow up once I finished high school, he wanted me to attend college and I wanted to make money. We bumped heads, he put me out my brother was already on the street hustling, when he cut off money from us I picked up the street life. I told her I was making more money in a day then my father did in a month.

For a couple of years I was on my own, the fast cash I became addicted too. My mother always snuck Kem and me home cooked food. We missed her cooking and nurturing. But our ego's was bigger back then and we felt we were men so we stuck together on the street. Kem had an opportunity to go out of state and take over some spots and he did that, leaving me on up here to handle the business.

Once one of my man's got murdered over a deal that went bad, I was so hurt I went to my father one night and cried to him. He didn't turn his back on me. He talked to me for hours about how real men are to be. He told me that this life was going to lead me where my man was, or in prison. He said, 'I will either be carried by six or judged by twelve', but it wouldn't end well.

I had more than enough money, cars and chicks for a lifetime. I was well known on the street, I was poisoning my community instead of helping it. My father called his brother my uncle Albert up and he joined in talking and ministering to me for weeks.

They had me watch documentaries of the Black Panther movement. They took me to places where my people were buried how my great grandfather died for fighting for what he believed in. They gave me books to read about black on black crimes how we destroy our own people.

They told me how hard they had it and how my father worked hard to keep his business. How blessed he felt when God gave him two healthy sons, that he knew one day would take over his business and keep it going.

My father gave me an ultimatum to get out the streets while I was still free, because he would never visit me in a jail or my grave. It stung my heart to hear him say it but it was the best thing he ever said to me. It was that night I decided to change my life. Six months later my father was dead. That's when my life changed forever.

Lacy listened intensely and hugged me tight.

"You make so much sense to me now Wolfe", and she held me until we fell asleep.

Her phone rang and woke us up. She jumped up and get herself together, and then I walked her to her car. We were in love and I felt good about that. I was opening up to her more and more. I was hurt she was leaving but I had a bigger picture to look forward to.

Once she left after kissing me like we were teens sneaking around, I watched her car disappear down the road.

My phone rang it was Sash, "Talk to me".

"Big Wolfe what you doing, still with pretty brown eyes?" Sash joked.

"Nah, what's up?"

"Kem is here with us, we coming over".

"What you punks coming by for, I joked?" I could use the company I thought to myself.

"Just to chill and eat up your food man, you know how we do maybe bust your ass in some pool or play station", Sash replied.

"Yawl negros didn't eat enough at the little party at shop tonight", I asked Sash.

"Man, we grown men, we ready to eat again", Sash laughed.

I shook my head, "I'm here".

"We on our way", he said and hung up.

I straightened up some; Lacy did the dishes and cleaned the kitchen before she left. It was plenty of food left over. I kept the containers out so they can eat but put a plate away for me I know how greedy those fools can be. Plus it was food from Mrs. Wilson left.

"Who the hell cooked this for you Wolfe, it was good as hell", Pete asked once they arrived they ate all the left over's.

"Lacy", I said.

"What? Brown eyes can cook too. I see why you not letting her go", Pete joked.

"Yeah mama is waiting on them babies too", Kem chimed in sipping his corona.

I shot him a look.

"So what's really good with brown eyes?" Sash asked seriously.

"I'm not telling you fools nothing about her beside she's my lady and that's it", I said looking at Sash.

"Oh any other chick, we can get the 411, so she's the one that got past that heart", Pete stated.

Pete knew more than Kem and Sash at this time. I wasn't going to discuss Lacy with them. Plus I didn't have it all figured out, "Clean up y'all shit, that's what y'all focus on right now, not my lady or business", I said in arrogance.

"This dude is serious right now", Pete pointed at me.

I walked into the living room and started up the play station. Kem sat next to me and we started playing NBA2K and of course I started busting his ass.

Sash and Pete joined us and witnessed the total ass whipping I was giving Kem. I looked at Pete and saw he was here but his mind was elsewhere. We laughed and bugged out all night. We joked on Pete and how he was caught cheating for the 100th time.

We talked about the shops and the future of some of the things we can do to improve. We argued over the best rapper out. Pete filled us in on how some chick saying he was the father to her baby. Kem told us that he had three chicks he was juggling and that's a headache. We joked and told him he trying to make up for all that time in jail.

Kem filled us in on some of the things he encountered on the inside. I shook my head. My heart ached for my older brother. He was better emotionally now but I know that was hard for him. He never wants to talk about our father a lot; he still feels the sting of his death.

Apart of Kem resented me because he felt my pops gave me more attention and love than he got. He never held it against me on the surface but I can see it in him. My mother also favored me, that I seen clearly. But my love for my brother was never questioned. I told him that I am here for him no matter what. He knew that. He saw my success; he envied it but benefited from it also.

I always felt he was much more handsome than I was, but as I got older we about the same. That is why I let him handle his own shop, we all in it but he controls the decisions as long as he makes the right ones. His problem is, is that he made poor choices and never wanted to listen to reason, now that he is older and see it's a right way of doing things he's doing better. I will always be here for him no matter what.

It would have been easy to have him move in with me but he needed to learn his own way and have his own space. I needed to situate things with Lacy, if anyone was moving in, it was her and ShyAnn. I had to win this little girl over, but regardless I knew deep inside that she was either going to gravitate to me or not. If she's anything like her mom then it will be okay.

Sash and Kem left after a couple of hours and Pete stayed around. I was curious to know why he didn't bounce with them but I didn't question it, I can use the company. Once Pete and I finished our last game on the XBOX, I opened him and myself another corona. Pete was my right hand man; we have been friends since we were kids. He knew my pops real well and calls my mother, mom.

Pete's upbringing was rough. He lost his mother and father early. Both his parents were big drug dealers in the area, leaving Pete and his sister with their grandmother to raise them. Pete was twelve when his parents were murdered.

His grandmother couldn't control him from that point; his anger drove him to the streets. He was a fighter, he had fights all during school and the streets feared him. He started running with a crew that was rough, he wasn't that rough but it was the only family besides mine that he knew.

145

I kept talking to Pete as kids assuring him that things would get better. My father was like his father, but it didn't replace his parents. Pete was loyal to me from childhood, he admired my strength he told me once but he had a lot of heart and if I got into any beef with anyone he would take care of it. I told him that I didn't need him to fight my battles, he knew that but he felt that my future was brighter than his so if something went down he would take the fall instead of me. Pete started working for me in the street which was my advantage because he was so feared.

We made money, went to all the clubs and was well respected. He never wanted to get involved in the shops but I taught him the business anyway, explaining to him that I just want him to check on each shop, teach him the ropes to any barber, let his presence be known. He knows how to cut hair, he's not great at it but if he had to fill in at any given time he would.

After Kem was locked up Pete left the game and opened up a bodega on the west side, it's not all legit but it's better than him on the streets completely. He is financially established and sticks close to me because he don't trust too many other dudes out here.

I told Pete the whole shit with Lacy, I needed someone to talk to and he knew from the first day I met her. He didn't think I should play in that area, he called it messy but he knew I was going to do what I wanted. He knows the females we ran through in our lives, and he now understands the love I have for Lacy and will be by my side regardless.

Pete sat still looking straight ahead; I knew he had something heavy on his mind. "What's up with you Pete?" I asked him putting my corona down.

Pete took a deep breath, "I heard some shit today that is bugging me the fuck out", he said rubbing his head as if he had a sudden headache.

"Ok and what was the news you heard?" I asked curious to know.

"You know that chick Nadia that I was fucking from Edgewood?" He asked me with his eyes wide open.

"Yeah I remember Shorty with the big ass, and red hair, she's pretty as hell", I replied.

"Yeah well I'm going to stay away from pretty bitches, word on the street that this bitch is HIV positive and going around giving it to every dude she fuck", he said pissed.

I picked my corona up and took a sip; I looked at Pete in surprised hoping this conversation wasn't going to go where I thought it was. I cleared my throat, "Ok and you wrapped your shit up fucking with her, right?"

He was silent, that silence pierced through me, "Pete man, what's up I know you didn't hit that bitch raw", I asked in disbelief.

"Man Wolfe, the first few times I wrapped up but the last couple of times we fucked—no go", he said and put his head in his hands.

I was speechless. I didn't know what to say to my friend as he sat here with this fucked up news, "Yo, Pete my pops schooled us on using condoms since we were ten, that's the code of the streets you can't tell me that you fuck without them".

"I know Wolfe, I know this shit man. All the drinking and smoking clouded my judgment I'm just scared as hell man I can't go out with the bug", he said.

I took a deep breath, and needed to think of something that was going to help my friend feel better somehow. I couldn't just dig the knife in any deeper he was already hurting, "Ok that's the word on the street, you need to get tested ASAP Pete", I said to him seriously.

"I'm scared Wolfe, I don't know what I would do if those tests come back positive", he said.

Pete's face looked heavy with worry, I never seen him like this before, "I love Lacy man, I do but I strap up all the time. She clean, she smell good all the time but it's just some chances as a man I'm not going to take".

Pete looked at me.

"Look man, I don't want to make you feel no worse, so let's just set an appointment up for you tomorrow at the doctor's office, the sooner you find out your results the better".

"I don't know about that Wolfe, I'm only 39 year old man", he replied.

Pete buried his face between his legs and for the first time ever, I saw my dude cry. I went and sat down next to him, "Listen Pete man, I'm with you- I will call and set up the appointment and take you—whatever it comes out to be we will deal with it however we got to I promise you that". I put my hand on his shoulder

Pete was silent as he lifted up his head up and stared straight ahead. I couldn't imagine what he was thinking.

My heart was heavy right now, this is my boy forever to think of this shit happening to him had my head fucked up.

"I'm going to kill that bitch if she gave me that shit Wolfe I'm telling you right now", he spat.

I didn't respond to that, because I know I would feel the same way, "Listen Pete, first of all this here is between you and me never worry about no one knowing your business, but as a friend I want you go and find out first before you make any moves on that bitch".

I got up to make us stronger drinks. This shit was too heavy for just a corona's. I handed Pete his drink. A Hennessy straight and I swallowed mines down in one gulp.

"I ain't ready to die Wolfe, for real", Pete sounded defeated.

"Pete to even think about having that shit can kill some of us, but in today's' world it's a lot of technology and medicines that's not going to take you out like that son, I promise you"

Pete took a deep breath, "Make that call for me Wolfe", Pete said.

"Done, tomorrow I'm all over it stay the night here in one of the spare bedrooms you need to just chill and don't need to be alone right now".

Pete looked at me and took another gulp of his drink, "Yeah you right, I'm going to chill here for the night", he said and sat back on the couch.

"Yo, whatever it is I got you one hundred percent my dude, know that", I said.

"I know Wolfe, that's why I'm here".

Pete and I kicked it for the rest of the night until he went upstairs to go to sleep. I sat up thinking about my life. It just made more sense to be with Lacy, all these females out here is loose. Life is crazy one day you living one way and then a sentence can change your life. I know that whatever happens with this Pete he was my man and I wasn't going to turn my back on him. I looked through my phone and made sure I had the doctor's number. That was going to be my first phone call when I woke up.

When I laid down, I thought of Lacy her face in my mind made me fall asleep without so much heaviness from Pete's news.

LACY

Romeo

Bradley came home Tuesday night, he was just as normal as I guess I be when I come back from one of my escapades with Wolfe. He was all over me, I was surprised but I couldn't reciprocate like I use to now knowing his news. He felt my coldness, I tried to play it off with him but I couldn't.

When he was asking me what the matter was, I just told him that I had my period and I wasn't feeling really good. I wanted to ask him a lot of questions about his business trip, try to see how many lies he was going to tell me but I saved myself the disgrace of it because I really didn't care.

He was upstairs helping ShyAnn with her homework while I was finishing up our dinner. I wanted to tell him about the location I was looking at for my studio, but I know that he didn't care too much about my work. I had to think of something to talk to him about because I didn't want to get to silent on him, he would know something was up. I know I made up my mind that I was not going to have sex with him. Wolfe was filling me up well in that department so I had no desire for Bradley.

After we ate dinner, I went to give ShyAnn her bath and put her bed when I came downstairs Bradley was sitting on the couch watching the news. He wasn't a sports fan which always made me wonder because every man I knew was a diehard sports fan for one sport or the other. He was more political and likes to know what was going on in world. I went and sat in my favorite plush chair and was looking at some papers for my next client. The house was quiet.

"So when do you think we should make the date for?" Bradley spoke out of nowhere.

"A date for what?" I asked confused.

"Our wedding date, it would have to be after my sister's wedding of course my parents keep asking me when we will at least set a date", Bradley said throwing me off.

I looked at him in disbelief; I had no answer for him. I didn't want to say the wrong thing so I just shrugged my shoulders.

"That's not an answer Lacy, come on now", he said, sounding frustrated.

At this moment the room felt so much smaller than it was, I just looked at him and kept quiet.

"What's the matter, you don't want to marry anymore?" he asked surprised.

"Honestly Bradley I am trying to open my studio and my clientele has gotten to be a lot, I haven't really thought about getting married any time soon", I said as honest as I could.

"I see", was his only response.

My insides was on fire, I didn't get it if you are cheating and this woman Tracy loves you the way she said she does, so much so that you invited her to your sister's wedding, why in the hell do you want to get married I thought to myself.

"I understand that you're busy, but we can at least set a date, and then I can tell my parents so they can lay off of me for awhile", he asked not getting the hint to leave it alone for now.

I looked at this man like he was crazy as a bat out of hell, something was up I didn't know exactly what it was but something just wasn't right, "Well I have no idea at this time, if you want to make up a date and tell them by all means do so but right now I have no idea", I said plainly. I felt him staring at me, as I looked harder in at my papers to not show my true aggravation.

"You know you are a beautiful woman Lacy", he said.

I looked at him. This was the first time he ever said that to me. Wolfe has called me beautiful more times than I can count, but Bradley hardly passes a compliment over to me especially in the privacy of our home. Now in public he would adore me, but here and now I was really shocked. I didn't respond to him.

"I know men tell you that all the time, don't they", he said with a smirk on his face.

I again just looked at him. Now I'm feeling like he may know about Wolfe and not telling me. This shit is getting too complicated I had to play mind guessing games with this man and it was becoming weary.

" To tell you the truth Bradley I don't pay attention to when men speak to me, I'm a photographer and mother, I don't go out that much and the men at the coffee shop don't pay too much attention to me at all", I said sarcastically.

He chuckled, "Well if they don't I do", he said teasing.

I could have gotten up and slapped his face, where the hell is all of this coming from I thought to myself? My cell phone buzzed I didn't look at it right away.

"You know I have been thinking that we should take a vacation, you and me and ShyAnn, it's been awhile since we all went away together, maybe we can take Shy to Disneyworld after

Layne's wedding", Bradley said watching me as I looked at my phone.

I looked at my cell phone it was Wolfe, the text read (missing you like crazy) I melted.

I ignored Bradley's question and thought it was a good time to tell him my plan about taking ShyAnn away for the weekend, "Since we are on the subject, next weekend Melissa and I are going to take ShyAnn away to Lake Success before she starts summer camp, just a girl's thing", I said casually.

Bradley looked back at the television, "She would love that", he said changing the channel from the news.

He became quiet which made me think that, that left him to scheme on his next lover's rendezvous.

I sent Wolfe a text message (I want to see you☺).

Wolfe texted back (I'm coming to get you now).

I texted him (No tomorrow I will be at your house by 9:00a.m.).

Wolfe texted back (I'll be waiting).

I texted Wolfe (double hearts).

Inside I was smiling, I haven't seen Wolfe since I cooked him dinner at his house. I missed him. We would call each other every day but he's been so busy and so have I. But I needed to be held and kissed and sucked and fucked real good another day couldn't go by.

What Man-Man and the community did for Wolfe showed me so much that night. This man was a real man. He was smart, giving, and loving and all about his business. People recognized him for his gift and loyalty. And his mother was so sweet; I see why he loves her so much. She kept telling me that I was the one so I assumed she didn't know my circumstances. Wolfe don't talk about it, he be about it.

The China situation was making me feel some sort of way but I can't dare feel sour about a situation that was going on before I came around. But the problem is she just going to go away? The night at the hotel party she was set on showing the world that she was with Wolfe and that just pisses me off. We had lives before each other, we just got to know our positions and hang on until it's all said and done. Wolfe was much stronger at this, than I was. Women are emotional beings, China may not walk away so easy. But that's Wolfe's problem to deal with for now. She will become my problem once I am done with Bradley.

Wolfe wasn't the typical man out here, he had something special about him, take away his money and fancy cars and house and businesses, he was special within and that is what I love about him. The way he looks at me, and handles me is like no man has ever given me that fire before. He goes out of his way to make sure that I am happy and taken care of.

I don't want to let emotions get in the way of my decisions because next year he could be a psycho, but then again so can I. I didn't even think about ShyAnn and me living with Wolfe. I don't know if I am going to do that yet, or am I going to just get an apartment or condo for ShyAnn and me until I get to know Wolfe more. I don't want to drag her from place to place but I'd rather be safe than sorry.

I think tomorrow I will start looking. My credit is excellent so I don't have any worries on that end. I have to think things through though, and see how all this plays out. My mind rushed to what I was going to wear to see my lover.

Melissa have been giving tips on what's sexy and not too revealing to wear. This is all new for me; I mean dressing up hasn't been my thing. I know how to when it's occasion but I'm use to my comfortable sweats and sneakers. I guess I have gotten so use to them that I forgot how to be sexy.

Melissa is coming by Friday to go over how to do make up and some clothes that she said will look great on me for my shape and size. She is so good with fashion I couldn't resist. Who I am with Bradley I will not be with Wolfe. Wolfe makes me feel sexy so I want to fit the part, plus I like when he sees me and his eyes light up. Melissa talked me into this when she knew we was going to the cabin with ShyAnn, she said that I had to look the part, she said that it's a way that we can put on sweats and a hoodie or flip flops and jean skirt with a t shirt and look sexy. I keep my hair up in a ponytail in the summer month's way too hot to wear down.

Melissa said she has different styles I can do beside a ponytail that keeps my hair off my shoulders and still look nice. I was excited to learn about beauty, she has wanted to do this for a long time. Bradley took me out my thoughts.

"I would like to take us out for dinner tomorrow Lacy", he said.

I looked at him again, "Well I have meetings all day tomorrow; I should be home by 7:00p.m. Mrs. Krauss will be taking care of ShyAnn until you get home, she's really doing us a favor watching her until she starts summer camp", I said.

"Ok then, meet me downtown by 7:30p.m. After getting Shy and we will make a night of it", he said satisfied.

I thought to myself this woman must really be giving it to him good. I went upstairs to take a shower and think about my lover, I was excited.

I got Wolfe's house a little after 9:00a.m. He had the door open for me. When I walked in his cleaning lady was cleaning the refrigerator out, I said hello to her and went to the living room where Wolfe was on the phone in an intense conversation. I kissed him on the cheek not wanting to interrupt him.

I took my sandals off and scooted next to him not wanting invade his conversation. He kissed the top of my head and started rubbing my back gently. I was looking around his house trying to picture Shy Ann and me living here. Wolfe's kitchen is like no other, I saw myself there. I was smiling without realizing Wolfe had gotten off the phone.

"Hey baby girl", he said and came to me and kissed me deep.

Yes, his kisses were inviting. I wanted to devour him right there but I had to keep in mind his cleaning lady was here. I wiped the lipstick off his lips.

"You look good baby girl and smell even better", he said as he was kissing my neck.

He felt so good, so strong; I was rubbing his back slowly, "Thank you baby", I replied with my eyes closed enjoying the soft kisses he was giving me.

Wolfe stopped and just starting looking at me like he never saw me before.

"What's up Wolfe, you okay baby?" I asked rubbing his head.

"You're so beautiful to me Lace, I never want to lose you again", he said with sincerity.

"Never baby, I'm here always", I assured him while rubbing his head close to my chest.

"You hungry?" he asked me.

"I am now that you mentioned it", I said sounding excited.

"I know a great place that serves breakfast, let me take you and then we can come back here and make love", he said with a smirk.

"That sounds good baby", I said as we kissed.

"I'm all done Mr. Harris", the cleaning lady stuck her head in the living room, smiling when she saw us kissing.

We stopped and Wolfe got up to gave her a white envelope that was sitting on the table.

We got up and started out to get this delicious breakfast that Wolfe was talking about. He hasn't been wrong yet with food, so when he said its good I trust him. I work out a lot more now because this man just feeds me and feeds me. Truth is he spoils me, and it feels damn good.

Of course Wolfe was right, we went to a diner on the north side of the city and the food was excellent I ate an omelet and turkey bacon with fruit salad it was delicious.

Wolfe seemed like he had some things on his mind, "Hey baby you okay" I asked him concerned.

Wolfe took a deep breath, "I'm good baby girl, nothing to bother you with just a lot of shit with the business is all", he said, then quickly changed the subject, "So next weekend it is", Wolfe said smiling. He was so handsome of a man I can never get tired looking at him.

"Yes, and I am excited and scared at the same time", I said with my lips poked out.

Wolfe grabbed my hands, "Don't worry baby-girl, it's going to be all good, we'll click you'll see", Wolfe said confidently.

"I'm sure", I said smiling.

"So I am going to plan a nice weekend for us, you have to write down some stuff for me so I can have everything ready when we get there", he said.

I knew the things that Wolfe meant, he mentioned to me before. He wanted to know ShyAnn's shoe size and clothe size, what her favorite character was, and her favorite color. I could only imagine what he was going to do.

"I have it here in my wallet", I pulled out a yellow piece of paper and passed it him. Wolfe pulled out his phone and took a picture of the list.

"I could have just sent it you in a text", I said.

He was busy on his phone, "What are you doing?" I asked.

"Sending it to Karen, she is going to make all the arrangements that she and I discussed", he said smiling.

"Oh, don't go spoiling her Wolfe she will get use to it", I said to him.

"I'm going to spoil her and you too", he winked at me.

At that moment I wanted him more than ever. He hasn't even met Shy yet don't even know how this is going to go but he giving, giving, giving.

"I want to do something special for you Wolfe, you have done so much for me and given me so many things; things that are special", I said looking at him intensely.

"Hey, you don't owe me nothing baby girl. I love you and I will always take care of you-know that", he said.

We finished up our food and made it to his house; I stripped myself naked leaving a trail of my clothes from his front door throughout his living room, to his bedroom. He was watching with eyes of a hungry lion wanting to devour me. I enjoyed teasing him. Wolfe took off all his clothes and stood before me like a black knight, I was embellished with his beauty. He was a gorgeous man.

"Come to me my love, let me make you a happy man", I said seductively.

Wolfe approached me and kissed me from head to toe, he sucked my toes and licked up my legs I was in pleasureville, and it was no feeling like it. My pussy was getting wetter and wetter, he landed between my legs pleasing my wet pussy with his tongue, I didn't want to reach an orgasm like that, and I wanted to feel him inside of me. Wolfe placed a condom on him quickly and entered me, I moaned loudly, he kissed and sucked my neck, and he was looking me in my eyes intensely. He loved me.

His moans reminded me of porn that I watch from time to time. My hands massaged his wide back, my legs wrapped around his thick frame perfectly. It felt so good, he kissed me deep, I sucked his bottom lip, he pumped me harder, as he pumped me I pumped back, we was in a rhythm that I never experienced before.

He moaned more, and I tightened my muscles, he moaned deeper in my ear, "I love you baby girl, he whispered in my ear".

I became wetter.

I licked his neck and gently bit his shoulder. Wolfe stayed inside of me for awhile, each pump felt better than the last, he turned me over I was on all fours, my ass up in the air. He was fucking me so good at this point, I was ready to cum.

I spoke it out loud, and he pumped harder and faster. I screamed in pleasure, I felt my insides exploding, it was a slow lasting orgasm, Wolfe started to cum as he pumped my juices was finishing and I enjoyed him cumming as he grunted and moaned.

I fell to my stomach, my legs were weak, my body felt like toxins was released in my body, and I felt refreshed. He kissed my backside, and gently bit it he then kissed my back. I turned around and kissed him deep, "I love you, Mr. Harris".

We took a shower together and laid naked in his bed, "I don't want to leave", I said quietly.

"I don't want you to leave", he whispered back as he held me tight.

We fell asleep in each other arms and woke up two hours later. I still had a few hours before I had to leave to pick up ShyAnn and meet Bradley downtown.

"So your girl that you was with that night at the hotel, she mess with Sash I hear", he asked as we laid in the bed cuddling.

"Yes, she likes him and understands her position", I said.

"I'm not going to ask what that means", Wolfe said.

"We should double date one day", I said.

Wolfe kissed the back of my neck, "Whatever you want baby girl, set a date and we'll be there", he stated.

"I will".

"Your girl like pretty boys I see", Wolfe chuckled.

"As long as they treat her right, Melissa will hang. She's about her business and takes no shit. She keeps her feelings in check, she don't let no man violate her feelings or space. She's strong", I boldly stated.

"Yeah well then she's a good match for Sash, he needs some taming", Wolfe joked.

"Well he got the right one with Melissa, she's a shield and handles herself well", I said confidently.

I told Wolfe how Melissa and I became friends years ago. He listened to me and we laughed and joked about how men and women are so different. I was schooling him on how women can much smarter in the game of life, he didn't agree but we agreed to disagree. I jumped up out his arms and hit him with his goose down pillow.

"Oh a pillow fight you want?" he jumped up smiling.

We hit and played with those pillows until we were both out of breath, his hits was so gentle I almost wanted to tell him but I knew he didn't want to hurt me. We ended by him pending me down on the bed and making passionate love to me again. I was game.

It was time for me to go; I had gotten dressed and was putting my lip gloss on in his bathroom. He stood behind me looking at me apply.

"You good?" I asked him smiling at him.

"I'm more than good with you, I hate to see you go though", Wolfe said not taking his eyes off my lips.

"I know baby but this is just for a time", I assured him.

"I have something for you", Wolfe said as I cut his bathroom light off.

He handed me a credit card, "Wolfe, what's this?"

"It's a credit card with a $5,000 limit, buy you something nice", he said handing me the blue card with his name 'Christopher Harris' engraved in it.

I held the card in my hand in disbelief, "Oh no Wolfe, this isn't necessary I have enough you don't have to do this". I reached out my hand to give him the card back.

"Lace, take the card for real I'm not taking it back. I want you use it for you and ShyAnn. Let me do this for you please".

"But Wolfe, I'm good I have enough", I told him confidently.

"Lace, take it", he insisted.

I gave up. His look of determination was too intense I wasn't going to win. I took the card and put it in my wallet, "You are way too much", I said as I got up and hugged him.

"Nothing is too much for my lady, it's nothing", Wolfe said.

I was thinking that this man is really going to spoil every ounce of me. Shy Ann's father tried to spoil me. He was a minor street hustler, he hustled credit cards and did shady things trying to give me the best he could. He died trying to hustler a street hustler that gunned him down over $1,000. The thoughts made me sad. Wolfe was all the man I needed.

"The very best for you Lacy, only the very best", Wolfe whispered in my ear.

He walked me to my car, we kissed and I said goodbye.

"It's see you later, Lace-Goodbye mean forever", he corrected me.

"See you later love", I corrected myself and chuckled.

As I was driving to get ShyAnn, I laughed out loud. I am one lucky woman with a twisted ass life. I had a couple of more places to check out for my studio. I called Mikey to set a meeting with him. He assured me he will be there. He was such a good kid, and just as passionate about pictures as I am. I was going to offer him a full time position as my assistant photographer and a place at the gallery once I found the location. I then will have to find a secretary to handle all the paperwork at the gallery and my private shoots. In my head it was coming all together. I was excited. I had all this work to do, plus this twisted love life I was living.

Wolfe and ShyAnn made my life worth living. I know whatever Wolfe had planned was going to be something wonderful, he never slips up. At the traffic light, I gently pinched myself because I wanted to know that this was real life and not a dream. I can't believe he gave me a credit card. I was use to being financially taken care of by Bradley. I guess I would never have to spend any of my money, which made that better for me because I can leave a legacy to my children. Yeah I plan on having more, and I will give Wolfe as many kids as he likes.

My emotions were on fire. I called Melissa, told her I would take her to lunch, wanted to fill her in on my latest drama. She agreed and was happy. I wanted this dinner to go quickly with Bradley. I didn't know how long I was going to be able to hold out on him. I wasn't in love with him, now I don't think I like him. I have nerve to feel this but this is how I am feeling. I am just as wrong as he is, but I'm entitled to my feelings and that is how it is right now. I probably won't see Wolfe again until we meet at the cabin, which was okay although I would miss him, I had something to look forward to and that kept each day for me full with expectation.

Melissa and I met at a restaurant downtown to eat lunch, then she's coming back to the house with me and fashion me up. Melissa looked like a little girl with a pink short jumper on, a pair of white tennis shoes, and her hair pulled back in a ponytail. Her purse of course matched her outfit. She looked beautiful. Melissa was a co owner of a small boutique in middle town, clothes and fashion was her thing.

"So girlfriend what's the 411?" she asked excitedly.

We sat down at our table and gave our drink orders

I had a huge smile on my face.

"That smile say Wolfe all over it", she said happily.

"Yes it does", I replied taking a sip of my drink.

I filled Melissa in on all areas of my life. She talked to me about Sash and that she is really feeling him. She knows that he's a major player but she insists that those are the type she likes. She can play while they are playing. Melissa was in a long term relationship with a man that dogged her out. Once she left him, she vowed to not get serious with any man until she fulfilled herself on every level. I understood that, if Bradley didn't come along then I would probably be too scared to have someone in my life also. It's easy to become guarded once your heart is broken so badly.

"A credit card girl that is some real life Romeo shit. That man is a keeper and the sooner you get exclusive with him the better it will be", Melissa stated smiling.

"I know that's right", I agreed.

I wanted to tell Melissa about Bradley's secret life too but I couldn't. I wanted to be clear about my decisions and didn't want anyone in my head. This was my life at the end of the day although I trusted Melissa's aggressive advice; I had to be silent on this one.

"Well girl you work that shit, and let that man give you the world if he wants too, you deserve it Lace; look I am not the one to ever want to break up someone's happy home you know that, but you deserve love, to feel love and be loved and Bradley somehow isn't doing that for you anymore Lace, I just want you to be happy and I seen you with Wolfe, I never seen you so happy", Melissa said.

I took a deep breath, "Yeah you're right Mel. But you know to love Wolfe is just easy for me, it's as if were soul mates", I explained.

"Yeah fuck mates' makes better since", Melissa joked.

"Real funny Mel" I snapped.

We finished off lunch and made it back to my house. The clothes that Mel brought was really nice. I looked cuter and cuter with each outfit I put on. I was amazed how a change of hair and a little make up with a nice outfit can change your whole attitude.

"You have the cutest shape", Mel said as she watched me in the mirror.

"Oh please, not nicer than yours, you're so curvy", I chimed.

"Well that's nice of you, it's different strokes for different folks, we are beautiful to God so what man thinks really don't count", Melissa joked.

"I agree", I stated as I turned around to check out my backside.

"Is it me or does my butt look rounder?" I asked Mel in seriousness.

"With all that good dick you getting I'm not surprised, you're going to have a K Michele booty soon you keep it up", Mel joked.

I looked at her like she was crazy, "You're so silly Mel".

We sipped some coronas and talked like we were teenagers. It was nice having Mel around and exhaling some of the shit on my mind. I know she felt the same way. I ended off with five cute summer outfits and some sandals and sneakers she brought me. Melissa wouldn't let me pay her for nothing. I didn't expect she would but I offered her because I don't take advantage of people. I told Mel about double dating. She agreed we would when I came back from the cabin. I started packing Shy and my clothes, I didn't want to wait to the last minute we were leaving out tomorrow night so I wanted to get started so when it was time to go we would just leave out.

As ShyAnn and I was on the road I started a conversation with her trying to prepare her for the weekend ahead of us. I wanted her to meet Wolfe and I wanted to prepare her some before he just walks in and she becomes confused.

Finally Friday morning came and I was making sure I didn't forget anything for ShyAnn or me. Wolfe was going to meet us there; he had some work to finish up before getting on the road. I was excited and scared at the same time. I told ShyAnn once we were in the car that we were going to a nice cabin and she was going to have a lot of fun. I told her that she was going to meet my friend. She was just so excited to be going somewhere.

"Hey Shy, when we get to the cabin it's a friend of mine that I want you to meet", I said, looking through my rearview mirror at her.

"Ok mommy, it's a friend like God mommy Melissa?" She asked.

"Yeah it is but it's a man and not a woman", I said.

"Oh ok, he's your friend?" ShyAnn asked.

"Yes he is and he's really a nice man, so I want you to be nice okay?"

"Of course mommy, what is his name"? She asked curiously.

"Wolfe", I said.

ShyAnn started chuckling, "That's a funny name mommy, Wolfe" she repeated.

I giggled at her.

"Is that his real name?" She asked.

"No ShyAnn, I'm going to let him tell you his real name okay", I said conspirely.

"Okay", she said innocently.

"We are going to have fun", I said.

"I wish Brad Brad was coming", she said sadly.

My heart stopped, I should have expected it but I put a smile on my face, "Yeah me too, but you will have fun with Wolfe, you'll see", I said trying to assure her.

ShyAnn continued looking out the window like she never road in a car before, she was paying attention to scenery. The ride was quiet, Shy Ann fell asleep and I turned up my music to put me in a good frame of mind. My heart ached for her, but I remember Melissa telling me that Shy will be fine. She's a smart and she's strong. Bradley went to work before we left. He went and said goodbye to Shy Ann before he left. As he walked out the door, I looked at him no hugs no kisses was exchanged. I just let it be, I had bigger fish to fry and he wasn't one of them right now. I just wanted this to be over, but I knew that time was of essence so I just put my patient hat on and chilled out.

I haven't found a studio yet, Wolfe said he will go with me next week to look at some locations that his people have available. I was grateful because the hunt was starting to wear me down.

Mikey is doing two shoots for me this weekend. The clients didn't' care that he was my assistant they just wanted their occasion covered. Mikey is great and professional I had no worries about his work. I knew when I returned that we will proof their packages and complete them when I returned. Everything seemed so exciting about my future yet so scary.

I was solid with Wolfe besides with ShyAnn and then I had to think about Bradley when we returned. If this weekend turns out like, I like I should be gone out of the house by the end of the month. It was summer time and I wanted to get settled into wherever we go before school started for ShyAnn in September. It was just a lot to do but I was confident all will work out well.

We pulled up in front of the cabin. To my surprise Wolfe's truck was parked out front. I was nervous I didn't think that he would be here; he said that he would be running late. This means I have no more coaching to do with Shy, it was do or die. I called his phone he picked up first ring.

"Hey, you here I see we are outside she fell asleep", I said and took a deep breath.

"Ok I'm coming out now", he said.

I sat still and talked myself into calming down, because this was going to be ok. Wolfe came out like a stud. His jeans shorts was crisp, his all white t shirt and all white uptown sneakers matched accordingly. His hair was cut nicely and his face was glowing. I wanted him right then and there.

"Hey baby girl", he said as he kissed me deep.

He looked in the back seat and stared at ShyAnn for a minute, "She's beautiful like her mother, a little princess", he said smiling.

He looked at me with a serious glare, "Hey" he said holding my face with both his hands, "This is going to be good, you hear me", he assured me.

"Yes sir", I said and got out.

I went to wake up ShyAnn as Wolfe started taking our luggage out of the trunk, "Wake up sleepy head, we are here now", I said touching her tummy through her pink sundress.

ShyAnn opened her eyes confused where she was and seeing her surroundings was different, "We here mommy, where's Wolfe?" she asked like she knew him already.

"He's right there", I pointed in his direction toward the trunk.

Their eyes met for a minute, they looked at each other like old friends, "You are the famous ShyAnn I see nice to meet you", Wolfe said as he approached her side of the jeep.

"I'm not famous", she said with a wide smile.

"You are famous to me", Wolfe said bowing to her. She started giggling.

"You're funny Wolfe", she said smiling.

Wolfe laughed out loud, "You are beautiful like your mommy".

"Thank you Wolfe", ShyAnn replied.

"Can I ask you a question?" she asked Wolfe.

"You can ask me anything you like", Wolfe said.

"What's your real name?" she asked innocently.

"Good question, my real name is Christopher Harris", Wolfe said leaning on the car giving ShyAnn his full attention.

"I like Wolfe better", ShyAnn said.

We both laughed, "Ok then, Wolfe it is to you", he said and put his hand out to help her out the truck.

"I have a surprise for you ShyAnn", Wolfe said walking with her and two bags out the trunk.

Wolfe whispered to me, "I see those pretty brown eyes runs in the family".

I smiled at him, "yes they do".

We walked in and it was nice and cool, Wolfe set the air once he came in. Wolfe put my bags in our room and took us up to the spare room where Shy Ann will be sleeping.

I was shocked to see that the whole room was done in pink and white, a brand new princess bed with matching bureau and mirror. A pink and white tea set table set in the middle of the room on top of a pink and white area rug. The wall was full of brand new toys neatly put aligned the wall. Everything I put on that list was in the room of the toys that she liked. The closet was filled with different outfits.

ShyAnn's eyes opened so wide, "Is this my bedroom Wolfe?" She asked excitedly.

"Yes it is and everything in is yours", he said proudly.

I looked at him and smiled; (too much) I lipped him. He waved me away.

"Can I play with my toys now", she asked.

"Of course you can, mommy and I will be downstairs", Wolfe said.

"Excuse me young lady, what do you say to Wolfe", I stared at her hard.

"Oh thank you Wolfe, thank you so much", she said and hugged his leg.

Wolfe knelt down to meet her eye to eye, "whatever you want is yours", Wolfe said to her and gently pinched her nose.

ShyAnn smiled and shook her head; she went to her toys and started playing with them.

"We will be downstairs Shy, you come down whenever you like okay", I said to her.

She was engulfed with her new things, "Ok mommy", was all I got.

Before we could get to our bedroom I stood looking at him, "What?" he said with a sly smirk on his face.

"Wolfe, you didn't have to do all of that, my goodness you are going to spoil her rotten, and you aren't suppose to buy her, just be you".

"Baby girl I am being me, that's what I do. The first impression is the most important now that I have her undivided attention the rest will be easy", he said confidently.

"I guess you're right, she's excited and happy thank you baby", I said kissing him.

"I told you I am going to take care of you both, and I mean it", he said seriously looking me in my eyes.

"Now let me get a good look at my lady", he said spinning me around.

I had on and orange tube top dress with matching sandals one of the outfits Melissa picked out for me, "You look good enough to eat Lace", he said with sex in his eyes.

"We have to be discrete Wolfe, I want you bad, but after we put her to bed tonight", I assured him.

"I know, I know", he whispered in my ear and kissed my neck.

"I don't want to give her so much, so fast in due time she will understand", I said rubbing his back.

"I can wait forever for you, but tonight is even better", he joked.

"So I have a good agenda set up for us, Karen helped me out a lot", he said.

"Oh yeah Karen, I will remember to thank her, I don't think she likes me so much", I stated looking at him.

"Who K, she cool she just knew about the letter is all and she's protective, she doesn't want to see me hurt", Wolfe stated.

"Oh so you told her about the letter hey, that's makes since why she spoke to me that way at the shop", I said.

"Yes and no, but she knows now to be nice and I won't allow disrespect towards you at all from anyone", he said seriously.

I laughed, "Okay bodyguard", and gently slapped his shoulder.

"Nah I'm for real, I am to protect you at all cost and that's what I do no one is to hurt you emotionally, physically, or any other way or they will deal with me", he said picking me up.

"Wolfe", I screeched as he spun me around and put me down then kissed my forehead. I knew what he was saying was true, he's a protector over the ones he loves and don't know. He was a man in every aspect. He made you feel protected and loved, I couldn't ask for anything more. He reminded me of my dad. That day he came and rescued me from my mother he promised me that I would never have to endure such things again and that he would always protect and love me.

The refrigerator was packed with all the stuff we liked and loved, it was a different comforter on our bed, then the last time we were here and the cabin seemed so clean and fresh. I haven't been here in the summer before and the central air was inviting it was at least ninety degrees outside, sunny. This was going to be fun.

Things were working out better than I expected. Wolfe went over the agenda; we would spend the day in town so ShyAnn can swim. I wanted to swim too; it was hot enough so we will make a day of it. Tomorrow Wolfe set up horseback riding, and going to the aquarium which is only minutes from town on the out skirts. Sunday we was going to the town's carnival and summer bar-b-q with all the other kids and games there I'm sure ShyAnn will enjoy herself. I was excited that this man thought of us so much to make each day full of fun just for my daughter.

He was who I was going to be with hands down. I was happy for the first time in a long time. Things just seem to working out. I know I had to still deal with Bradley but this was by far my biggest obstacle. Once this weekend was over it was time to start making plans to start making moves.

After we came from the pool, we were exhausted. Wolfe still has enough energy to start the grill outside in the front under the shaded tree. He grilled hot dogs and hamburgers, steak and corn on the cob. It was all seasoned in a large pan which tells me that he had someone season it and put it in the refrigerator. I wasn't mad though I was hungry and just happy I didn't have to cook. ShyAnn and I went inside to take a shower and change our clothes. When we came out our color deepened from the sun from the pool. ShyAnn's fair skin turned light brown. She was so cute with her jean short set and tennis shoes I brought her.

"Hey Wolfe want to play a game with me", she asked him.

I looked at him, "Okay, what game is this?" Wolfe asked her smiling.

"Animal play", she said innocently.

"Animal play? You have to teach me that one", Wolfe said gently pinching her nose.

"It's easy we go through the whole alphabet and have to name an animal that starts with the letter, I will start A for alligator", ShyAnn said with her knowledge.

"Oh that's easy", Wolfe said.

"B for bear", he said confidently.

They went on and on, so I went inside to make some phone calls. I called Melissa first I wanted to inform her so far how things are going, "Hey Mel it's me".

"Hey girl, how's it going", she asked.

"Better than I expected, she loves Wolfe", I beamed through the phone.

"Of course she does, who doesn't", Melissa chuckled.

"No seriously, he hooked a bedroom up for her. Any little girl would fall in love with. It was laced with toys all pink and white...girl he must have spent a fortune".

"Well he should, you are her mama he gave you 5,000 without thinking so this isn't anything to him Lace. Listen let him spoil her, whatever it takes to get yawl pass this season. He's doing the right thing you just have to learn to embrace it without standing in the way", Melissa said.

"Yeah, yeah you're right Mel, as usual", I chimed.

"Well, look you guys enjoy and call me when your back in the city. I will cook us some food and we will chat it up", she said.

"Sounds good, make sure it's healthy I've been eating like a pig since Wolfe came into my life", I laughed.

"Yeah ok, tell your tiny waist that it seems like it has a mind of its own. The more you eat, the smaller it gets", Melissa joked.

"Ha, ha" I said to my crazy friend, "Love you Mel".

"Love you too girl, see you soon and tell that fine man of yours I said hello".

"I will", I laughed, "later silly".

The night went well, we ate together inside at the table. I looked at us and saw my future sitting in front of me. Wolfe and Shy was engaged in a conversation about SpongeBob. I looked at Wolfe and thought he's an incredible man and I am lucky. I had things set ahead of me but I was willing to do whatever it took to receive the happiness I knew I finally deserved.

Our last night at the cabin Wolfe made passionate love to me, we were quiet to not wake Shy but it was different for me I was glad our bedroom downstairs and she was upstairs. She snuggled in her new bed feeling like a real princess. I felt connected to him in a way I never did before. I know him meeting with Shy had a lot to do with those emotions.

The next morning Wolfe was bringing the bags to my car, I had a bitter sweet feeling over me. I was elated that Shy liked Wolfe, and sad because I knew I had to deal with some stuff to make this right. It was time to say goodbye to the man that I loved.

"You're beautiful", Wolfe said standing by my truck, making me blush.

"Thank you baby", I said smiling.

"So this went well", Wolfe said smiling.

"Yes, thank the Lord now I got work to do when I get back", I said taking a deep breath.

"Yeah you do baby girl, but we almost there" .

"Yes we are", I smiled.

"Hey ShyAnn take good care of your mommy for me okay", Wolfe said as he looked back in the truck. He walked over to her and gently pinched her nose.

"I will Wolfe" ShyAnn replied smiling.

ShyAnn had a bag of toys and clothes that she wanted to take with her and Wolfe granted to her with no problem.

Once we said our goodbye's ShyAnn and I was on the road, Wolfe and I agreed I will come over by the end of the week. I knew he would text me daily to hold me over. Once Shy and I was on the road my thoughts were racing.

ShyAnn interrupted my thoughts, "Mommy do you like Wolfe more than Brad Brad", she asked.

I was quiet for a moment I had to think about my response, "Why do ask that?"

"Because you smile a lot with Wolfe and not Brad Brad", she said plainly.

"Ummm, it's a different kind of like mommy has for Wolfe than Brad Brad", I explained.

"You love Brad Brad, but like Wolfe", she asked.

"Well I love them both, in different ways", I tried to explain.

"Will I see Wolfe again?" she asked.

"Yes I'm sure".

She smiled

"Shy I want you to do me a favor", I said.

"Yes mommy", ShyAnn said.

"Until mommy figure some things out I don't want you to mention Wolfe to Brad Brad just yet okay?"

"Why?" she asked curious.

"Just for a little while, I will let you know when you can but right now you can tell Brad Brad everything about the trip just leave Wolfe out for now okay?"

"Ok mommy", she said still confused.

"Thanks sweet pea", I said feeling horrible telling her to do that, but I needed to cover all bases so I can handle this situation accordingly.

I saw our future looking bright so I am going to trust in believe that to be true with doubt.

WOLFE

Bad News

I stayed at the cabin a little while when Lacy and ShyAnn left. I had to make some phone calls. I was worried about Pete results but wasn't going to worry too much about them until they came back official. I took him the next morning he spent the night at my house.

This man that I knew was scared and I felt every ounce of it. I kept assuring him that things were going to work out. It did little for his state of mind but I knew my presence with him helped him along.

The weekend went well. I had no doubt that I can be a positive male figure in Shy Ann's life. She was beautiful, smart, and witty like her mother. I didn't exactly know what Lacy's plan was for walking away from her situation but she seemed like she had things under control. I just couldn't wait to have all of her.

I was doing my work also, ignoring every text message I received from the random females I was dealing with. It wasn't as hard as I expected. My heart was filled with Lacy it wasn't enough room for anyone else at this point. Plus, with Pete's situation it was an eye opener for me to just fall back. When I needed sex Lacy provided and that was good enough for me at this point.

On my ride back to the city my thoughts went to the information Lacy told me about her mom a few weeks ago. I could never imagine having to go through that as a child. My parents were so close that I couldn't relate to her pain. It hurt me to hear about her early childhood, but it made her such an amazing woman. And she's a great mom to ShyAnn. She isn't her mother at all at least from my angle and that alone she should be proud of.

I was meeting with Kem at my crib he and I had some business to discuss about the shop. I loved my brother but I didn't share as much information with him as I did with Pete.

Distance formed between us when he was locked up. Although we are grown men and connect I know that he still harbors resentment towards me and I love him but kept some things to myself. Kem arrived ten minutes after I walked through the door. I was sorting through my mail.

Kem had a key to my house, I heard him come through the door, "Little brother" he said walking in.

"What's up brother", I said and fist bumped him.

I looked at my brother and seen my pops. People say I favored my mother with my complexion and thickness, and my brother took after my father's fair complexion and height.

After we went over some minor details on the shop Kem was in charge of, we went to the living room to relax and drink ice cold coronas.

"So playa what's up with brown eyes?" Kem asked.

"Ain't nothing, that's my lady we good", I assured him.

"Lucky man", he held his corona in the air.

"Yeah man she's dope but what's up with you and these females out here?" I asked him.

"Man ain't shit, you know a different one every night", he laughed.

I looked at him remembering Pete's situation, "Aye Yo, you strap up with these chicks right Kem", I asked him concerned.

He looked at me puzzled, "Hell yeah man, you know pops taught us that shit young. I don't take any chances with these females out here", he said confidently.

I felt relieved.

"Why you asking for anyway?" he asked.

"Nah just making sure you know, you were locked up for a minute just want to make you ain't forget the codes of the street, because some of these chicks got game", I said.

"Yeah well game or no game I ain't no fool, I know what's up out here", he stated confidently.

"That's what's up"

"Yo, Pete seem a little weird to you lately", he asked.

"Who Pete, nah you know Pete he in and out at times but he cool", I said as assuring as I could.

"Yeah well he don't seem cool lately he just be having this look on his face sometime when I see him is all", Kem said as he took a swig of his beer.

"Yeah well you know he got the bodega, and he hit the shops every day for me so it could be a combination of things, I wouldn't worry about him", I said.

"Nah I'm just asking I know yawl tight".

"Yeah Pete's my man", I changed the subject real quick, "Yeah but these females is something else", I said.

"Speaking about females what's up with China, seen her the other day she was salty, a little cold. She was looking good as shit though", he laughed.

"Yeah she bitter right now, but she'll be alright", I said trying to brush her off.

"Wolfe the heartbreaker", he saluted.

"Man please these females know what time it is from Jump Street, if they feelings get hurt it's because they be all in them. I lead none of them on, it is what it is", I stated defensively.

"Not brown eyes though, she pierced an arrow right thru your heart and stopped that Casanova bullshit", he laughed.

I shot him a look, he was right but I wasn't going to give him that satisfaction.

"I'm not mad though, we been in these streets for a minute it may be time to look for a Shorty to settle down with", he added.

"That's grown man talking right there", I said and raised my corona up

Kem and I kicked it for awhile. It was refreshing talking to my brother. We talked about my pops, laughing at our childhood memories. It's nothing like vibing with my brother; we were best friends before we had friends. I want us to get closer like we were as kids. My father instilled the importance of family and brotherhood to us daily.

Kem left a few hours later, I was ready to walk out of my door to take care of some business and Pete was standing there about to ring the doorbell.

"Pete man what's up?" I could tell by the look on his face it wasn't good news. My heart started to speed up.

"Ain't good Wolfe", he stated looking defeated.

I let him in, he looked a wreck. He had no haircut; an overgrown beard was pasted on his face. His eyes was bloodshot red, he was a mess. We sat on my couch; I cut the air back on. Pete reached in his pocket and passed me the paper in his hands it was the results of his HIV results that read **POSITIVE.**

My heart ached for my friend. I stared at the paper for a minute and took a deep breath, "Yo, Pete man I'm sorry about this shit".

"I'm going to kill that bitch Wolfe, tonight", he said with a fire in his eyes I never seen before.

"Yo Pete I get it for real, but think about it man you kill that girl. You in jail the rest of your life man", I said trying to reason with him.

"I'm already dead", he yelled.

"Calm down Pete".

He sat back and started crying. I went to get him tissues. I had to think about what the hell to do. I knew for a fact that Pete would kill that girl and I couldn't let that happen. I had to think quickly. I went into my bathroom and I looked in the medicine cabinet. I had sleeping pills in there, he needed to sleep and he wasn't going to sleep with this news so I had to force his rest. He was going to need it. I came back with a glass of water and two small white pills.

"What's this?" He asked.

"Just take them, they will help you relax then I want you to go upstairs and take a shower and lay down Pete, this is a lot to digest. You don't need to be alone right now. I'm going to figure this shit out", I said pissed off.

Pete just looked at me, "I'm going to die man, straight like that bruh. I'm going to kill that bitch".

"Take these", I put the pills in his hands and gave him the water he swallowed in one gulp.

"Look Pete I got you one hundred percent, but you got to listen to me. Do what I say do and we gonna make it through this shit, yah feel me?" Pete looked at me like a lost child.

"Yeah man, I feel you", he said sounding defeated.

"So go upstairs, lay down you need some rest when the last time you slept?"

"Two days ago", he said and looked it.

"Yeah you need to go lay down. I'm here but you need strength and sleep will help you", I said.

"Thanks Wolfe"

We fist bumped and Pete walked slowly up the stairs. I had to think of something quick. I couldn't change the results of that test but I could stop him from murdering that chick. I pasted back and forth then I had an idea. I picked up my phone and went to work.

One hour later, Karen came through the door that I left open; I didn't want her to ring the bell and wake Pete. He was sound asleep when I went to check on him. I didn't tell Karen the truth about Pete I made up another story and she went for it.

I needed her to make arrangements to get Pete to Florida to the summer house down there. It was my father's property he left to my brother and me along with his barbershop. We go there every summer. Its right on the water and Pete can use a getaway right now just to get his thoughts together. I called the maintenance down there to make sure that it's clean and tidy for him.

Karen agreed to take him there and make sure he was situated before she leaves. Karen got started on her phone making sure his flight was secured; I called Sash and asked him to go to Pete's crib and get whatever clothes he had and pack them up. He didn't ask me any questions.

Once Karen and I finished setting up for Pete's trip. Sash got to my crib with his things, I asked Sash to stick around to give Pete a haircut before he left, so he chilled with me. Karen left to take care of her business, I was once again grateful for her friendship and loyalty to me.

We moved around like soldiers, when one of us was hurting, we all was hurting. I told Sash the same story I told Karen, (Some chick came up pregnant trying to pen the baby on Pete and get him for his money, and added a death of one of his cousins to make it more potent). They didn't ask too many questions which was a relief to me but I wasn't finished with my lies to them.

I went to my bureau took out my stash and put $7,500 dollars in cash in a yellow envelope and sealed it. It was for Pete to use while he was in Florida.

It was midnight before Pete woke up, Sash and I was playing the Xbox, I had to act as normal as I could. I couldn't give off the sense that I was in pain over my friend's situation. I heard movement upstairs and wanted to talk to Pete before he encountered Sash. I wanted to reassure him that I had his back tell him the story I made up for him. I had to assure him that Florida was the best bet for now, how he needed to get away and think, changes his environment. I told him everything has already been taking care of and his flight leaves in the morning. He was hungry, he looked better than he did earlier. The pills worked allowing him to sleep.

I had ordered him a cheeseburger deluxe because he needed to eat. He ate all of it. I assured him Sash or no one else knew the truth. Sash started cutting his hair after he ate. He didn't' question Pete about his situation the code is, we'll talk when we're ready. Pete looked like a new man once Sash was done.

The weariness still sat on his face but it was lighter. I told Pete to take a shower clean his self up he did as I instructed. I gave him my new basketball shorts I just brought and a clean t-shirt, and some white socks. He looked better.

Sash cleaned up the hair put everything away and we sat playing Xbox, laughing and joking on each other. Pete was looking better and feeling better, I felt good about that. Once Sash left, Pete went to bed he had an early flight to catch. As he was walking up the stairs he stopped

"Hey Wolfe".

"What's good Pete?"

"Thanks, Man".

"We family Pete, we family no thanks required".

Pete smiled and walked upstairs. I shot Lacy a text, I wanted her here with me but I couldn't force the issue. I wanted to feel her, smell her, and touch her. This news about Pete was fucking with me but I knew he would be alright. I went to my laptop and printed all the information on HIV that I could and printed it out. I wanted Pete to read that it's an incurable disease but treatment and medication was available that he can relatively a healthy life. I didn't know what else to do. If I was him I would be fucked up in my head too. But we got to keep moving regardless, I wasn't going to let him slip. I was going to walk with him each step of the way.

The next night

I wasn't supposed to see Lacy for a couple of days but I texted her and asked her to call me. She called me immediately; I explained to her the situation with Pete. I had to lie to her too, my word was bond with Pete and I couldn't break that even for the woman I loved. She came to me.

I left the door open for her, when she walked in I was in the process of finishing my pushups. The stress of Pete's news was weighing down on me. It could have been any of us to trip up like that. Lacy walked in looking good as hell. I wasn't expecting her so quickly but when she arrived I was smiling inside. She sat down and watched me finish up, I blew her a kiss, and she caught it. I went to take a shower, I was dripping with sweat. When I came out, she made a drink and we sat intertwined with one another on the couch. The house was quiet, I was content.

"So you sent Pete to Florida?" she said quietly.

"Yeah it was best to do, he's in bad shape", I said.

"Life is funny though, you never know which way it's going to go", she said rubbing my hand.

"That's about right Lace", I took a deep breath knowing the truth about Pete.

"Wolfe you're a good man, you take care of everyone around you. Not many people would do the things that you do for people", Lacy said while stroking my hand.

"Yeah well I'm blessed, I've lost and gained all through life now I'm at a point where I can look out for people and that's what I do. My pops use to tell me to ain't nothing wrong with taking care of people when you love them and even better when you don't know them".

"Wow, I see your dad was a good man too, he did well by you and Kem. Every young man should stand on that foundation it would make the world a better place". She kissed my hand.

"Yeah my pops was old school, he was a loving man but he carried this confidence that intrigued people especially men, owning his shop gave him opportunity to school a lot of men in his day while they got their hair cut, and my friends also", I stared straight ahead.

"Priceless", Lacy said.

Lacy and I laid there awhile before she started kissing me deep. I needed to bust a nut, I took her bra off and she slipped her panties down. I sucked her nipples while she massaged my dick. It felt so good. We gave each other head, I wanted to cum right there, but I wanted to be inside of her.

Once I placed the condom on, I turned her over and had her from the back with slow strokes, I undid her hair clip and let her hair fall past her shoulders, grabbed her hips. She wanted to be fucked today, not made love too. I gave her what she wanted.

I pumped inside her while she screamed my name in between the sexiest moans I ever heard before. Her head rotated back and forth giving me more pleasure. She was sexual, she enjoyed being pleased and in return would please me just as much. Once we were done we laid up.

My phone rang, it was Pete, "What's up Pete?"

"Hey Wolfe just checking in man", he said sounding better.

"You okay down there?" I asked as I sat up.

"Yeah man, wake up to blue water and the sound of the ocean. I watched a lot of comedy last night to make me laugh. I'm doing some writing, shit like that", Pete said with a chuckle.

"Good, good, that's what you need".

"You know Wolfe I been doing a lot of thinking, I was a fucking fool. I knew the risk of fucking that chick with no condom and did it anyway", he said.

The phone was quiet and I felt the need to fill the silence, "Listen man do not focus on that shit, try to think good thoughts. Everything up here is good. Sash, Karen and Kem take turns checking on the bodega and picking up your money. I don't want you to worry".

"Man, I know you got me. You my best friend, you always come thru for me. This one was big though. My thoughts didn't change for wanting to bury that bitch", he said getting hyped up.

I changed the subject.

"So K left you the Dr's name and phone number that you will be seeing down there", I got up and walked into the kitchen.

"Yeah I got all of that, thanks", Pete said.

"That's what we do. So listen I'm gonna holler at you later on. Stay up", I said.

"Yo Wolfe man, any talk going on up there?"

"Nah man, nothing on the street, I would tell you". I lied I would not have told him if it was. I wouldn't want to make him feel any worse. He needed his peace of mind. I haven't heard anything yet. Just the lie I told was circulating about in a couple of shops. Pete knew a lot of people.

"Cool".

"So later we'll talk" I said, "Peace"

I hung up my phone and stood at the sink to digest our conversation. Pete's not letting up on killing that chick. I'm just glad he out of sight and shit. I took a deep breath

Lacy came into the kitchen and hugged me from the back, "You okay baby?" she asked.

"Yeah, I'm good baby-girl"

"Wolfe, I'm ready to tell Bradley that I am leaving I already starting packing me and ShyAnn's things and leaving them in containers in my garage".

I stood still it was the news I needed to hear through the bullshit that was running across my mine with Pete. I turned around and hugged Lacy, "We can start bringing your stuff over during the day little by little", I said.

"That's the thing Wolfe, I'm leaving Bradley I already have a two bedroom apartment I signed a one year lease. It's in Melissa's building", Lacey said surprising me.

"What? Why can't you just move in here with me now Lace?"

"I mean I can, and I will, but not now. A one year lease is all I signed. Let's be together, enjoy each other, and date openly and after one year we'll make that move. I just want ShyAnn to digest you slowly. The building is where Melissa lives so I have a babysitter and I can spend as much time with you as I want. I will spend weekends with you. I thought this out in its entirety, it's just best for now baby".

She touched my face and I took a deep breath, "I don't agree. but I do understand, I just want you".

"And you will have me babe, but let's do things right. You are use to having your own space. A child in here will be a lot. Let's move in slow motion it will be best for us but I am yours".

"Ok, but one year", I assured her.

"One year", she agreed and put her pinky up to make a pinky promise.

I picked her up and sniffed her neck she was all I wanted. Lacy and I spoke more on how she was going to tell her situation that she was leaving. She said that she had it all planned out. She told me that his sister was getting married and she was going to go and take ShyAnn for his family.

ShyAnn was close with them and she wanted her to see them again before she walked away for good. It was mid week and they will be leaving out Friday and the wedding was on Saturday. Lacy said she would tell him Sunday morning before they flew back here. Tomorrow she will pick up her keys, and she was going to have her assistant start bringing their stuff to the condo from her garage. It was set in place and I was happy.

I still had Pete on my mind but I kept focused on the shops and Lacy and Shy Ann. Although they aren't moving in right now, I had one of my spare rooms set up for Shy Ann, the painters will paint it all pink and white and I will Karen put a touch of princess love in there like she did the cabin. I needed to show Lacy that I was ready for this. I see her mind is straight on what she wants and I can't blame her for that. I just want to prove to her that I love her, and her daughter and I am ready for this. I know that the transition won't be easy but Shy Ann is a smart girl, I will just spoil her and let her know that there is nothing that is too good for her. Lacy has pride and she's an independent woman. I don't know many women that would turn down money and luxuries but this is why I love her. I know she loves me for me and not what I can offer her.

The next day

I was sitting in my living room, the T.V. was on but I was going over some paperwork from the downtown shop. I haven't heard from Pete, I called K to see if she have spoken to him but she said she hasn't. I wasn't too worried; he was far away and in a content place. The last time I spoke to him I was sure that he was in a good frame of mind. I picked up the phone to call Pete at the house and it just rang. I tried his cell it went straight to voicemail.

As I hung up the phone, something caught my attention to the T.V. the anchor spoke "**Breaking news, a young woman was found strangled to death in her apartment last night in the Edgewood section. Her sister found her and called police. It was no forced entry, police assumed whoever committed this murder. There are no leads to her killer but the police are still investigating**".

I froze; it all had to replay in my mind again. The picture that they showed was Nadia the chick that gave Pete HIV. I put all the papers aside and tried to call Pete again and still there was no answer.

I stayed calm, I knew Pete was in Florida, maybe some other dude found out about Nadia's tactics and went and killed her. I didn't want to think that Pete was responsible for this. I brought him to Florida to avoid this. If it was her time to go then her karma came back on her. I'm sad for her family but I don't want Pete to get himself in trouble. He was like a brother to me.

I tried calling him again this time I left a message. I called Karen and asked her to keep trying Pete. I called Sash asked him did he hear from Peter he said not for a couple of days. I called Kem and he told me the same thing. Now I wouldn't be so worried if I could contact this dude. But I can't get in touch with him; this girl has come up murdered. It just wasn't feeling good to me. I called Karen and asked her to come over asap.

Karen arrived in less than thirty minutes, "What's going on Wolfe"? Karen asked with concern.

"I can't contact Pete I feel like something is wrong with him", I stated standing up.

"Ok, maybe he just wants to be alone I mean damn Wolfe you called me over here because you can't contact Pete, you must think I don't have shit else to do with my time bruh", Karen stated angrily.

"Karen, Pete is HIV Positive and the girl that gave it to him was found dead in her apartment last night. I just saw it on the news".

Karen sat down and had a look of terror on her face, "What"?

""That's why I sent him to Florida; he was threatening to kill that girl. I mean I can understand why but I wanted him to get him away to get his mind straight", I said and sat down and started rubbing my hands together.

"Damn Wolfe, you should have told me this before", Karen said.

"I couldn't K, my word was bond with him, I was all he had I had to stay loyal".

Karen shook her head and understood the code of your word it's all about trust, "This shit is fucked up", Karen said.

"Yeah tell me about it, and now no one can contact him, did he flee? Did he come back and killed her and left town? My mind is all over the place", I said angrily.

"Ok wait a minute Wolfe, calm down. We can sit here and go over a thousand things in our head but that's not going to help. What we are going to have to do is get to Florida on the next plane available", Karen said plainly.

I looked at her. She was right I can sit here and contemplate whatever I want in my head. If Pete's isn't answering the phone then we have to go there and see what's up with him.

"Book our flight K, whatever they have available we have to bounce", I got up.

"Ok I'm going to take care of that, pack a bag I'm going to go home and pack a bag and make these arrangements I will let you know when to come and get me, I'm going to try to get one for tonight", Karen said confidently.

I looked at Karen she was a beautiful woman inside and out. And next to my mom she was the strongest one too. She rarely let me down and just looks out for me however she can. She's a true friend and I needed her more now than ever.

"Thanks K", I said and opened my arms to hug her.

"You got it Wolfe. You know how it is when one is hurting we all are hurting. I just hope Pete is okay, maybe he left something in the house down there. Or maybe he is there and found him a girl", Karen said.

We both just stared at each other I saw pain in her eyes that I never seen before, we loved Pete he was our brother, "I will call you stay by your phone", Karen demanded and walked out the door.

Me and my driver picked up Karen at 6:00a.m. the next morning, and our flight left at 8:00a.m. That was the earliest that she could get for us. I tried Pete's phone all night and no answer. I was mentally drained. I barely had gotten any sleep. Florida was a three hour flight; I was hoping to sleep on the flight so I could deal with Pete accordingly once I found him.

Once we boarded the plane we sat in our first class seats and waited for takeoff. I had no appetite but Karen made me eat something. We sat in silence, both of our minds was racing with thoughts of turmoil. I called Lacy and told her that I had to go out of town on important business. She understood and I assured her that I will call her once I got settled. I knew she had her own stuff she was going through. It's amazing that when shit hits the fan, it all happens at once.

Karen looked at me, "Pete must have been scared to death when he got that news", she said.

"He was fucked up, he came to me in trust that I would help him and I did the best that I could", I said feeling like I let Pete down.

"You always do the best that you can for everyone around you Wolfe that's why people love you, for your selflessness. It's rare to find in men, most men are selfish bastards", she hissed.

"Yeah well I was when I was younger; you go through those stages in life. I'm just mature now K", I said.

"Even when you was a knuckle head out there, you still had a great heart", K said in sincerity.

I took a deep breath, "I remember when my father would have Pete and I sweep up the hair in the shop when we was kids, Pete use to hate it but he knew my father didn't take no shit. I use to laugh at the faces he would make, he would always dump hair on the floor and have to re sweep the shit", I chuckled.

"Yeah he was lazy as a child, no one taught him shit besides your dad so he wind up having his own store now", Karen replied.

"Yeah my pops always talked to us about life, looking back now it was all preparation for where we are now", I said thinking about those good times.

"Well that's the responsibility of a parent to prepare their child for what's out here", Karen stated.

"Pete sounded good last time I spoke to him, he was concerned about the streets and was they talking, I told him no because no one knew the truth but him and me", I declared.

"Yeah well his life changed overnight with that news and I'm sure he's just fucked up about it, I just hope he had nothing to do with that girl's murder", Karen said.

"She was out there spreading that shit around consciously K from what Pete said, some street dude was going to get to her sooner or later", I said hoping it was someone else and not my friend.

"Yeah well there's man's rules and there's God's rule most of us don't wait for God to do his work, but everything is going to be okay Wolfe", Karen assured me and squeezed my hand.

"Try to sleep. You look exhausted I will wake you when we are about to land", she said.

"What would I do without you?" I asked.

"Live", she stated and we both chuckled.

I put my head back and thought of Pete, and then I thought of Lacy and our new life together. My hope was that we get there and Pete was sitting outside looking out into the ocean. My mind was everywhere but I was just going to focus on what Karen said—everything will be okay.

Once we landed we rented a car and got to the house, I didn't have to go inside to know that Pete was dead. I told Karen to stay put in the car and I opened the door. Flies were everywhere. I covered my nose and walked to where I saw Pete was on the floor next to the table. He had a gunshot wound to his temple and the gun laid beside him.

I felt sick, my worse fear came true. I never mentioned to Karen that I thought he would kill himself. I was taught not to speak things into existence. I was crushed. I wanted to fall down, I stood looking at my dude pale my life will never be the same again.

I went back to car, "Call 911 Karen, he's dead", I said slowly.

"What…dead, what the fuck you mean?" she was terrified.

"Call 911", I screamed at her.

She picked up the phone without arguing and spoke to the dispatcher. The ambulance was there within minutes. I was numb Karen was silent when the police came I answered as many questions as I could, the area was filled with police cars and ambulances people were scurrying around doing their jobs.

A detective approached me at the car, "Are you Wolfe?" he asked with a white letter folded.

"The victim wrote this to you, it was clearly a suicide but after you read it I will need it back as a part of evidence", he stated.

I took the letter slowly, Karen watched me as I read it.

Wolfe,

I'm sorry dude about all of this shit. I know you did everything you could to help and I want you to know that I love you for that but I can't go on. I tried, I really did. My thoughts kept haunting me. I sat here day and night and couldn't get past it. My life was over; I did this shit to myself. That bitch got what she deserved but this ain't no life I want to live no more. Take the bodega and sell it, give some money to my cousins in the north and my aunt patty and uncle ray. You know where I keep my stash, keep that for yourself. Give all my things to good will, clothes and jewelry. Make sure it goes to people that can use them. I don't have much else. Burn me, keep my ashes with you. I don't want you to feel bad for me, I made my choices Wolfe. You did the best for me, no one in the world looked out for me the way you and your family did. I died knowing that!

Forgive me brother, I love you

Pete

Karen took the letter from me and read it, she started crying hysterically. I tried to hug her to calm her down but I couldn't. This was the first time in a long time I seen Karen cry in this way. I was so broken up in my heart. The detective took the letter from Karen and asked if we could come to the precinct to answer more questions. He told us to take our time and we needed it. I was weak and my friend was now weaker, I took a walk down the beach and Karen sat on the beach watching the water in silence.

The coroner came and took Pete's body out; it was all I needed to see before I broke down. The cool wind was soothing to my broken heart. I called Kem and Sash and told them the news, they we broken up. They was taking the next flight out to get here, I needed them now more than ever.

I tried calling Lacy and didn't get an answer. I wanted my baby right now I was fucked up. I couldn't get Pete's lifeless face out my head. My tears flowed. The water was calming and I walked so far I lost sight of Karen and the house behind me.

Two hours flew by before I realized that we had to head to the precinct. It was too much shit to think about right now, but I had to be strong. Once I finished up all the calls I sat for what seemed like eternity, I made my way back and Karen was in the same spot.

We comforted each other with sad smiles and assurances that we are going to make it through. I told her that Sash and Kem was on their way down. We stayed at the precinct for over three hours. We booked ourselves in the Hilton once we got our rooms Karen went to hers and took a nap. She needed it; her eyes were puffy and face was pale. I wanted to make her well but I was too broken myself.

I brought the pills that make you sleep and Karen didn't hesitate to take two. I took no medication, I left Karen's room and entered my suite and went straight to the bar. When I awoke my phone was ringing it was Kem.

"Hey Wolfe, we here now what room you in?"

I gave Kem my room number and they were up less than 10 minutes. I was foggy from the drinks I had earlier. I opened the door and hugged my brother like I never will see him again, then Sash and I hugged. They looked better than Karen and I did but you seen the pain on their faces.

We all sat in silence which seems forever, I made drinks for us and we sipped in the stillness of our silence. My head was all over the place. My heart was broken. Kem broke the silence and said that the word got out about Pete and it was buzzing around. I just listened, I knew from the news crew that someone was going to see it and start the buzz. I could care less, my friend was gone and what people were saying about it didn't concern me.

A part of me was angry at Pete, he could have called me and spoke to me about this. He could have done anything beside take himself out. My emotions were running. Sash spoke about the last time he spoke to Pete, and so did Kem. I sat listening, they didn't know the truth and I wasn't ready to tell them. I knew I had to; it had to make sense to them. I kept my loyalty to Pete, but he didn't keep his to me.

An hour later, I came clean about the truth with Pete. Kem and Sash stood staring at me, "That nasty bitch", Sash spat.

"That's some fucked up shit", Kem said shaking his head.

"It makes more sense now", Sash said rubbing his head.

"But who killed the bitch?" Kem asked.

No one knew that answer, it couldn't be Pete, and the time doesn't make sense. He was dead for over two days in the house. I'm guessing he hired some dudes to do the job and once they finished he took himself out. That makes more sense on time table.

"That bitch got what she deserved man, that's why I don't fuck these hoes with no condom. It's suicide if you do", Sash spat and we all agreed.

Kem stepped out to take a call; Sash and I spoke about bullshit trying to get our minds off of this nightmare. I tried Lacy again and still didn't get an answer. I see she left me a voicemail; she must have called while I was sleeping.

"Hey Wolfe, Its Lacy I am going to leave out one day early to get to the wedding. I wanted to spend the night with you before I left but when you had to go I decided to get this over with and give Shy Ann time to spend with his family, most of my stuff is packed. I am looking forward to being with you once I get back, love you baby and I hope all is well". Beep.

It was other messages from my mom and Man Man. Karen's girl left me a message, concerned she haven't heard from her since we left. I called her first to assure her Karen was okay a bit shaken up and I will have her call her when she wakes up.

I called my mom and Man-Man back. We all fell asleep, Sash was knocked out in the chair, and Kem lay across one of the Queen Size beds. We were all so emotionally drained. Karen was still asleep when we fell asleep.

I woke up to Karen's swollen face, she looked rested but weary, "Hey K, how you feeling?"

"I'm ok, better than I was and you how are you doing Wolfe?" she asked concerned in a whisper.

Kem and Sash was still knocked out, "I'm trying".

"Yeah this shit is heavy, but we need to eat. We got to stay strong through this. I will order room service for us all. I know what each of you like to eat, I'm glad they're here", she winked and looked at Sash and Kem.

I looked at my friend and seen the woman I knew. It was hard to see this pain in Karen. She loved us all. She was down for us; put us in our place when we would step out of line. And she back to taking care of us in spite of her sadness.

"Call your girl, she's worried", I stated.

"I will as soon as I call room service".

Karen told me that we would have to stay a couple of days because of the arrangements of getting Pete's body back home. We had unfortunate business to tend to down here. But we are his family so we got to do what we got to do. She assured me that she would make all arrangements once we got home to give Pete a respectful going away ceremony. This made me appreciate her loyalty and love even more. I needed her strength this was going to be a long and painful journey.

Two days later

We officially finished our business in Florida it was the longest two days of my life. All the arrangements were made to get Pete body shipped to our local funeral parlor and Karen made the arrangements with them. We were going to cremate him and have a memorial.

I spoke with his aunt briefly explaining I was going to take care of his funeral and finances. I let her know once the store was sold that I would distribute her fair amount and everyone else's that Pete said in his letter.

Karen had set up for a cleaning company to go to his apartment and clean and start packing all of his clothes so that we can decide where to donate them to local charities that are in need, I was thinking of a men's shelter. Although we accomplished a lot it was still a lot that needed to be done.

I finally contacted Lacy, her and Shy has just landed safely and she said that she will contact me once she settles in. I told her the news about Pete and she wanted to come to me right away. I told her not too, we were okay and I will see her when she returns. She didn't like my response but she didn't argue she knew I needed to do what I had to do and I had my support system around me. I love her with no doubts. When I heard her voice it was all that I needed to hear. I can't wait to see her.

Our flight was leaving tonight; the detective at the precinct assured me that once the investigation with Pete was closed that he would send me the letter. I wanted to hold on to it, it was his last thoughts. I decided that I would put it away in a safe place.

I sat in my suite alone before we were heading out to the airport. I looked around and closed my eyes. I kept seeing Pete, I would open my eyes and then close them, I would then see Lacy and Shy Ann smiling, I then saw my pops and moms laughing in our kitchen in the house we was raised in. I saw Kem and me playing ball as kids on the playground. I saw me and Pete sitting in my pops shop talking about the type of women we wanted to get. I thought about how life can change in the blink of an eye. Life was different for me now. My best friend is gone, yet the woman I love is freeing for me to give my all too. In these moments in life you have to think about the good things because if you stayed focused on the bullshit, your mind will go crazy!

LACY

Exposed

ShyAnn and I flew out a day before we was suppose to. I wanted to get this over with as fast as I could but I wanted to let ShyAnn say goodbye to the only family she really had. It was the right thing to do. I thought if Tracy showed up at this wedding I was going to pass the baton to her and give good reddens to the life I knew, with the man I thought I loved and loved me.

Once we got to the airport, I rented a car and we were off to Bradley's parent's house. On the drive there my thoughts went to if we would stay there, if it was my choice I would have gotten us a room at a hotel. I will see how the energy is before I make a solid decision. ShyAnn had kids that were expecting her and she was excited about that.

Bradley had a big family. They were prestigious people very well off and educated. On the outside they looked like the perfect family but I knew better. Bradley's dad was a retired sergeant from the navy and he ran his household the same way. Bradley's mother never worked, she was a nice looking woman to be in her 60's. Layne was a beautiful woman also and she was sweet. I see that her mother could poison her with some of her arrogant ways but Layne was much mild than her mother I hope that she grows into a more humble version. In the open they showed loved but you can see that words were passed when you weren't around. I could care less how they judge me, this was going to be a part of my past but I had to do things the right way in order for me to move on. I wanted to be fair to ShyAnn in this process.

I couldn't wait to see Wolfe, I am so sad to hear about Pete it all seemed so unbelievable. My baby was hurting I could feel his sadness on our last conversation. I wanted to run to him and help him the way he helped everyone else, he didn't allow me.

Truth was I had business to attend to so that when we got back home our new lives began. I knew that I had to comfort my lover and stand by him no matter what. Wolfe was strong, but death by suicide from our loved ones is devastating. My mother's sister Carol killed herself at the age of 25 and my mother never put the bottle down after that. My heart ached for Wolfe and his friends but I know that they will make it through with the tight love they have for one another.

I called Melissa and gave her news about Pete, Sash already informed her. I asked if she could watch ShyAnn when we got back. I wanted to stay with Wolfe as long as I could; I knew I wanted to spend at least a couple of nights with him when we returned. I cleared my calendar to make sure that nothing interrupted this time of mourning for him. I couldn't imagine not having Melissa in my life or for her to die so tragically. Tears welled up in my eyes and I sucked them in when I pulled up in front of Bradley's parent's house.

His parent's house was like a mini mansion, it had 6 bedrooms, a large corridor, a huge double sided kitchen, a game room, a sitting room, and all the furniture in it was modern and expensive. You could eat of the floors and they had more than enough space to for people stay over comfortable. Their living room was the size of my whole house.

The outside was pedicured perfectly with red and yellow roses blossoming in the front yard, two large lion statues sit at the front steps as if they were intimidating bodyguards. The water was on sprinkling the whole premise. It looked like a house from a movie. Again I found myself somewhere I didn't want to be, but I was doing what I had to do.

I opened the trunk; Layne's gift was in the back seat with Shy. I was surprised that it seemed so quiet, I wasn't sure if someone was home or not. I didn't see any cars in the driveway except a red Mercedes that I never seen before. I thought that maybe it was new car someone brought. I closed the trunk and thought again that I wanted to go in before I started taking our bags.

"We are at Ma and Pop Pop's house again", ShyAnn sang showing how excited she was.

"Yes, we are and I want you to be one your best behavior young lady", I said to her with a stern look.

"Yes mama I will be", she shook her head in agreement.

"That's my girl", I said and kissed her forehead.

We rang the bell and there was no answer. It was hot and my brow started to sweat. Seconds later a short stout Spanish woman with a maid uniform opened the door, "Hola, can I help you?"

I never saw her before. I assumed she was here helping with preparations to the wedding, "Hi, I'm Lacy and this is ShyAnn, I am Bradley's fiancé we are here for the wedding".

"Oh Miss Lacy, yes, yes come in please", she said as she ushered us in, "My name is Sofia, nice to meet you".

"Nice to meet you Sofia, I'm Lacy and this is my daughter ShyAnn it seems quiet where everyone at is?" We walked in and as I expected the place was spectacular, ivory roses sat around the corridor and living room.

"They all went to watch a play at the theater with Layne's fiancé's family", she said while maneuvering through the kitchen.

"Oh that's nice, did Bradley go?" I asked.

"No Mr. Bradley has room at the Hotel Plaza downtown". she stated.

Why is he staying at a hotel if his parents have all this room? Tracy was my initial thought. He was sneaky as I was I'm thinking.

"Hotel Plaza, Sofia can ShyAnn stay with you while I go downtown quickly, I want to surprise my fiancé". I asked keeping my emotions of anger intact.

"Sure she can…would you like some cookies and milk?" she asked ShyAnn

ShyAnn looked at me for the go ahead, "Yes you may", I smiled and kissed her.

"Mommy will be back soon baby", I said and kissed her on her cheek.

I found the address on my GPS and started out. Once I arrived at the hotel people were scurrying around. It was a five star hotel of course. I needed to get upstairs so that I can at least catch him in the act, put the letter I found in his hands, and walk away. No conversation would be needed. I had the man that I loved.

At the front desk the lady was nice but she told me that there were strict instructions left at the desk for this room to not be disturbed. I kindly smiled and asked her can she at least give me the room number. I'm sure they will come down and get me. Somehow that worked.

"Room 505", she stated with a smile.

"Thank you and have a great day", I said returning the smile.

I put my sun glasses on and made it to the elevators with a million thoughts running through my mind. I hit number 5 and waited patiently. I didn't know what the hell I was going to do I just kept moving. Once the elevators doors opened I walked around until I found the room. I walked past the room because I knew that cameras were throughout the hotel. I went into the stairwell to think of my next move. If I just knock that would make sense but did I want to see him with another woman?

I was no better than Bradley, I had no right to judge him but something in women makes them territorial and although I knew my wrong he would feel my wrath one way or another. He should not have asked me to come to this damn wedding; I should have declined, made up an excuse. But maybe something in me wanted to see Tracy, look at her and see what I didn't have. I don't know but if I continue to sit here it's just going to make things worse. I was going to knock on the door. I needed to get this over with.

I walked slowly to the door and put my sunglasses on the top of my head. My heart was palpating, and my hands were starting to sweat. I heard faint noises through the door, but nothing solid. I knocked twice. I heard movement. Then silence. I heard again movement again, I knocked twice again. A tall dark skin good looking man with no shirt and dress pants on opened the door. I became confused.

"I'm sorry is Bradley here?"

The man looked at me and then smile; I'm thinking I have the wrong room. That lady gave me the wrong room number oh God I look like an ass, "I'm sorry I"…

He interrupted, "No don't be sorry, Bradley is here".

He stepped aside and I walked into a huge master suite that smelled like used condoms and an unmade King size bed. Wine glasses on a table empty. An empty wine bottle, I was confused, it made no sense. I didn't see Bradley. My legs started to tremble.

"Brad, it's for you", the half naked man said in such a sinister way it made the hairs on my arms stand up.

Bradley walked out of a close door with no shirt and blue underwear on. I looked at Bradley then looked at half naked; the look on Bradley's face was indescribable.

"What the fuck is this?" I asked shaking.

"Lacey let me explain", Bradley said.

"Tracy I'm guessing, Tracy that wrote you this", I threw the letter at him.

Tracy stood with a sinister look on his face, "Your gay Bradley, you are fucking a man?"

"Lacey let me explain, please", Bradley pleaded.

I charged at him and got in his face, "You're going to explain what, that you have been fucking a man the entire time with me. That you are a homosexual and you then come and lay with me? What the fuck are you going to explain?"

I looked at Tracy in disgust, he wanted this to happen. He looked relieved if I could read him properly. I felt sick to my stomach. I am a fucked up person and I have been dishonest I get that much. But this man has been hiding a whole life from me, and sleeping with me. I felt light headed because I was doing the same.

"Lacey sit down, and let me explain", Bradley said, but I wasn't trying to hear him.

"No, you had five years to explain this crazy shit to me", I screamed to top my lungs.

Tracy remained standing with his arms folded with a sinister smirk on his face. I wanted to throw up. I couldn't get my thoughts straight, this shit had my mind scrabbled.

"I wanted to tell you Lacey, I did but..."

"But what motherfucker? WHAT? You're a down low brother that likes pussy and dick and you wanted to marry me, you wanted to bring me into this bullshit for that sake of what?" I screamed with drool coming out the side of my mouth. I was so pissed off and humiliated at the same damn time.

"No one would have understood, not you, not my parents", he said in defeat.

"Your parents, oh I get it so find a dumb needy woman like me to come and rescue, fuck men on the side, and live your life at the expense of my pussy and emotions, and my daughter", I stood still in my insanity and thought of our daughter.

ShyAnn asked me about two men being together, she must have found something or saw something. I charged at Bradley with all my might scratching and kicking, my sandal flew off, Tracy was behind me trying to pull me off of him, and Bradley let me hit him he didn't defend himself

"Get the fuck off of me!" I screamed.

"Leave her", Bradley told Tracy.

Tracy put his hands in the air, "I'm just going to leave you two to discuss this matter", Tracy stated like a real asshole and backed away.

I shot him a look of anger, my hair is wild and I'm out of breath, "I trusted you with my child, I let you take her places, you exposed her to this, I should kill you right here", I charged him again, and again he stood still. Tracy lifted me put me in the chair.

"Don't you touch me again you disgusting freak", I yelled.

I was out of breath, I started to cry not because of love lost but because I have been so naïve, so blinded. I exposed my child to this, I'm no better than my mother.

"Lacy I love you I do, I'm sorry", Bradley stated sadly.

"Love me, you don't love me. You used me, you set me up, you knew when you met me you like men. You gave me no options, just an emotional rollercoaster. You paid all the bills to cover your guilt. You lied; you were unemotional to me because you never wanted me", I said with tears in my eyes.

I picked up the one sandal on my foot and threw it at him, he ducked and it missed him. He started towards me, "Lacy please listen to me, I-"

"Shut the fuck up Bradley, I will be gone by time you get back. I closed out our joint account and kept your half in a yellow envelope in the bureau-have a nice fucking life", I got up in a zombie motion and walked out; I had no shoes on and didn't care. I couldn't cry I was too angry. When I got to elevator Bradley was in the hall.

"Lacy please let me tell my parents", he begged.

I looked at him, chuckled with my own sinister glare in my eyes shook my head in disbelief and stepped in the elevator with my bare feet

For some reason when I got off the elevator I was completely calm. I was numb, I had no emotion. I walked up to the same lady at front desk and asked her where I could buy a pair of shoes. She directed me to a boutique around the corner. I brought a pair of plain black flip flops and went to my car. My phone was ringing, it was Wolfe. I didn't want to answer it but I had to I needed him.

"Hello".

"Hey baby girl", Wolfe said.

"He's gay Wolfe, all this time he's been sleeping with a man", is all I could say.

"Who, your man?" Wolfe asked sounding surprised.

"Yep".

"Lacy where are you?" Wolfe asked.

"My daughter has been exposed, I'm no better than my mother", Tears started falling out of my eyes now.

"Lacy, tell me where you are baby girl I'm coming to get you", Wolfe said sounding like he was ready to come get me right now.

I told Wolfe slowly where I was in between my sobs and just sat there.

"Listen I am at the airport in Florida about to leave, I'm going to redirect this flight to you. Get you and ShyAnn somewhere safe baby. I'm on my way keep your phone on", Wolfe instructed.

"Okay" was all I could say.

I hung up the phone and sat mute for what seems hours. Thoughts and fears ran through my mind. What did my child see? How did I let this happen? This is the karma I get for being unfaithful! In five years I used condoms and birth control with Bradley but it was times we didn't.

Oh God I have to get test for all STD's and HIV. I was just tested three months ago; I'm going as soon as I get back. My mind was racing; I felt an anxiety attack coming on. I held the steering wheel and drank the warm water that was in the car. I wanted to call Melissa but she would come down too and I didn't want a disaster. Layne deserved to have a perfect wedding without any drama. I couldn't expose him to his family at this time when love was really in the air for Layne and her soon to be husband. I wanted too though, I wanted to punish him, I wanted him to suffer but I was just as guilty. Wolfe and I always wear condoms but he has to get tested too. I felt sick. I opened the car door and threw up.

Wolfe was coming to save me again, his best friend is dead and he's coming to rescue me. I should not have told him. I should have waited. I wasn't thinking. I tried calling his phone it went straight to voicemail. I was devastated. I can't keep interrupting people's lives.

I felt angry at myself for being blind and foolish. I knew Bradley and I was just two people living together, avoiding each other at every opportunity. I was just as guilty. I didn't want to think anymore. I put on the radio and let music try to soothe me. I put the air on in the car, I started to feel better. I started to cry again.

I must have cried myself to sleep and woke up to a knock on my window. It was a tall white man with blue eyes and a nice smile.

"You okay there"? He asked with a southern drool.

"Yeah I'm fine", I lied.

"Just checking I seen you been here from the time I went in and came out and that was hours ago".

"Oh shit what time is it", I cut the car on and it was after 6:00p.m., ShyAnn I thought, "I'm fine thank you so much" I said, put the car in gear and raced out the parking lot. I needed to go get ShyAnn and make up a good lie why we have to leave.

I reapplied my lip gloss and wiped under my eyes to make sure I looked presentable the first light I stopped at. I checked my phone Wolfe left a message.

'Hey Lace, my flight should arrive by 7:00p.m., meet me at the airport then', his message said.

Wolfe left the flight number and I had one hour before he landed. I was almost at the house hoping Bradley's family didn't arrive yet. I wasn't mentally prepared to be fake and phony. I can't blame them, he had them fooled too I guess. I just wanted to be normal. I was going to get my child make up an excuse that we will be back and never look back.

When I arrived at the house cars were all over the place, I panicked, "Shit, shit, shit," I yelled.

I didn't want to face these people. I couldn't. I knew they would do no harm to ShyAnn they loved her. That brought me comfort. I couldn't punish his whole family for this bullshit. I decided I was going to just call the house, speak to someone and wait to get Wolfe from the airport by myself. I needed him. I only had an hour to go. My hands were shaking.

"Hello".

"Hello, who is this" Janice Bradley's mom answered.

"Hi Janice, it's me Lacy", I said as normal as I could.

"Lacy love where are you? Are you with Bradley? ShyAnn is here having a ball with the other children", Janice said.

I heard kids laughing in the background, "Um no I'm not with Bradley, I will be there soon though, I went to meet him but we didn't connect", I lied.

"Oh well then take your time, you know I have to call that son of mine and give him the business about his tardiness, he knows that we are having dinner for the wedding party", she complained.

I was silent.

"Well Lacy, Layne is looking forward to seeing you my dear. Dinner starts at 8:00p.m. sharp", She informed me.

"Okay well may I speak with ShyAnn please?"

"Oh honey don't bother her, she's having a ball running around with the other kids, she'll see you when you get here", she said.

I took a deep breath and rolled my eyes, "Ok, see you soon".

"Goodbye dear".

I was lost. ShyAnn was fine. I drove around a little then I went to the airport and found a spot to sit before I went to arrivals. I just prayed that Wolfe's flight was on time.

I called Melissa I needed to tell her my truth, she was devastated.

"What the fuck…Lacy girl are you okay? I'm coming there", she demanded.

"No Mel, Wolfe will be here in 10 minutes I'm okay seriously. I love you and thank you but I promise you I am good", I begged.

"I would have got my child out of there", she spat.

"She's fine there Mel, they love Shy besides you they are all the family she knows. She's too young to remember my dad and she never knew my mother", my eyes welled up again.

"Lacy Grant you listen to me, you are a great mom-you hear me? A great mom and I don't care what the devil has set up for you God will save you. You are a strong woman and this will pass. You have your Romeo coming to rescue you again in his own turmoil, that man loves you girl- I love you".

I started to cry, my phone buzzed Wolfe was on the other line, "Mel its Wolfe I will call you as soon as I can, I love you girl" I said quickly.

"Ok go, love you too", and she blew me a kiss.

"Wolfe".

"Hey baby where you are?" he asked.

"I'm coming to arrival now, 10 seconds away".

I saw him with his duffle bag, looking good and welcoming. His face was heavy in his pain but he still looked good. In spite of it all he had that gorgeous smile. I jumped out of the car with a cab blowing behind me.

"Go around", Wolfe shouted.

I hugged him like I would never see him again. I was comforted by his tight embrace and body scent. I felt protected again. He was kissing the top of my head and my eyes was closed trying to prevent the tears from falling against his chest.

"Where's ShyAnn?" Wolfe asked.

"I left her at his parents' house; she's safe there I promise you I just couldn't get her in my condition", I confessed.

"I understand".

He looked me in my eyes, "You okay baby-girl?" holding my chin.

"I'm as good as I can be", I said with tears in my eyes.

An officer approached us, "Ma'am you can't stand here" he stated.

"We out", Wolfe said without looking at the man.

We got in the car and drove on side of the first park we saw, Wolfe was driving I didn't have the energy. We sat idle looking out into the park.

"Lacy look at me baby, I'm sorry this shit happened to you. Life is crazy when the shit hits the fan it hits the fan. But we are strong, we have each other now", he said gas he held my hand.

Tears started flowing again.

I told Wolfe the whole truth, when I found the letter. My intentions of catching Bradley and what happened at the hotel. I told him everything!

The look on his face told me that he shouldn't see Bradley any time soon. Wolfe took a deep breath and put his face in his hands.

"Wolfe baby you're in your own pain let me handle this. I'm so sorry" I said feeling overwhelmed by the whole situation.

Wolfe looked at me, "I am here to protect you, he will never hurt you again baby girl I promise you", he said looking at me intensely.

"This is my entire fault", I said it too quickly.

"Your fault, listen to me Lace don't put this shit on you. You had no idea about that man. You trusted him. Yeah you have your own shit to sit in-sit in that but don't put that man's issues on your table. He's a coward and twisted fuck", He said in anger.

I looked ahead at the light wind blowing against the trees in the mist of the sun setting. The sun was bright orange hovering over the trees in the park. Despite all the drama it was a beautiful scene, calming!

"Now what?" I asked Wolfe.

"Now we go and get ShyAnn and get the next flight out home so we can mend our hearts back together", Wolfe said slowly.

That sounded good to me, but home wasn't the home I knew. I have a new place, its new beginnings. I was excited about that but so scared in another. But I had Wolfe, I had Melissa, and Mrs. Krauss said she will always be there for me. I thought about how anxious I was in opening my new studio. I had so many things to get done but finding my peace of mind was first in line, I couldn't move further without it.

"You know we have to get tested for everything Wolfe", I said sadly.

"I know", was his only response.

I felt as if he was angry with me but he didn't show that. He showed love and concern as always. I was being paranoid, he didn't have to be angry with me I was furious with myself.

We pulled up in front of Bradley's family house. It seemed like even more cars was out there. I took a deep breath

"I'm going to go in and get her, I will be right out", I stated.

"If you're not out in 10 minutes, I'm coming in", Wolfe said ready to jump out of the car.

"Wolfe no, let his sister enjoy her time. I can't rob that from her because of this situation", I begged him.

"If you're not out in 10 minutes I'm coming to get you", Wolfe spoke and I knew this man was dead serious about what he was going to do if I didn't come out in 10 minutes.

I wasn't going to win this one. I opened the car door and made my way down the driveway. I didn't know if Bradley made it back here and didn't care. I was going to go in, get my child, throw my head back and burn that bridge once and for all.

When I walked in the door it was over 50 people scattered about. Everyone was infested in their conversations with wine glasses in their hands and classic music playing loudly. It was a perfect opportunity for me to find ShyAnn and get out without notice. Janice and Layne saw me before I could take two steps in.

"Lacy, you're here" Layne screeched running to me, looking beautiful with a teal dress and pumps to match, her makeup was perfect and hair was up in a bun.

"Layne you look absolutely beautiful", I said as we hugged.

"Thank you...You look good Lacy", she stated rubbing my right cheek.

I didn't respond

"Bradley is here Lacy, now where is he?" his mother said while hugging me short and quick as she was looked around the room.

"Um where is ShyAnn?" I asked quickly trying to make my move.

"In the game room with the other kids, Lacy are your okay honey", Layne asked with concern.

"Oh I'm just fine girl just jet lag is all", I lied.

"Excuse me", I said and walked off quickly.

I thought about Wolfe, he said 10 minutes. I knew he would be counting. I rushed past the uppity crowd in to the game room. Bradley was sitting down playing with ShyAnn she looked so happy.

"Hey Shy come here", I said smiling at her. I gave Bradley a look-that if looks could kill he would be dead.

"Hey mommy!" ShyAnn screamed and ran to me.

I hugged her so tight. I squatted down and hugged her so tight, then took a look into her eyes, "Listen we have to go now, I will explain everything to you in the car. But I need you to listen to me and move quickly ok", I touched her cheek.

"Are we coming back", she whined.

"Say goodbye to Bradley and let's go", I instructed.

She was confused, I felt horrible. But I couldn't deal with emotions right now Wolfe said 10 minutes.

I heard Bradley calling me through the music and laughter in the air. I ignored him and thought he may not want to come outside. We got to the front door, he was on my heels, "Lacy, let me talk to you please", he begged.

I turned around quickly with insanity in my eyes, "You-have-nothing-to-say-to-me, you understand me, nothing and if you don't want a scene in here you will let me walk out of here with my child in peace", I spat at him.

As soon as I opened the door Wolfe was standing there, "Everything okay", Wolfe asked.

Janice and Layne stood behind Bradley looking confused.

"Lacy where are you going with ShyAnn, what's going on here?"Janice asked.

"Lacy please what's wrong?" Layne pleaded next to her mother.

I looked at each of them slowly, then I stared at Bradley he had a look of panic on his face.

Wolfe was looking at me with his hands folded with the calmest look on his face and a slight smirk.

"Layne I'm so sorry, we cannot stay I apologize. I want you to go back inside and enjoy your dinner party please. Bradley will explain everything to you", I said as calm as I could.

Everyone looked at Bradley.

"Bye Brad Brad", ShyAnn said sadly.

"Lacy and I need to talk", Bradley stated and started towards me.

Wolfe stepped in front of me with his hands still folded his body language said what his mouth wouldn't.

"What's up bro?" Bradley asked confused.

"I'll tell you what's up you bitch ass motherfucker, I'm going to let your sister have her peace because Lacy asked me too but if you ever step foot near Lacy again I'm going to bust your asshole wide open—get it" Wolfe said in anger but laughed a sinister laugh looking Bradley square in the eye.

Bradley stepped back, "Let's go baby girl" Wolfe said and started walking away.

Bradley just stared at me. I grabbed ShyAnn's hand and caught up to Wolfe.

LACY

HEAVY HEARTS

After waiting around for our flight we were finally boarding. ShyAnn cried for over an hour she didn't understand what was going on. She sat on my lap and fell asleep. We sat in first class seats. Wolfe was staring into space.

I was afraid of what he was thinking as we sat there and he held onto my free hand. I didn't know if Wolfe and I were going to make it past this. I loved him and I know he loved me but so much happened in such a short time. He was my lover for over a year now he's my man and you don't know what a man is made of until turmoil shows up in their lives. I wasn't going to allow fear to overtake me. I made it through some dark times in my life and with or without this man I must know that I am going to be okay.

Wolfe must have reading my mind. He squeezed my hand and kissed my cheek. I knew my thoughts were wrong. Selfishly forgetting that this man just found his best friend dead by suicide, I had to adjust my thinking, he's in pain. I laid my head on his shoulder.

"I love you Lacy Grant" he whispered.

I smiled, "I love you more Mr. Harris" I said.

"Is she going to be alright" he asked looking at Shy.

"Yeah she will. I will have a good talk with her and she will adjust-she's strong".

"I'm going to take care of you both Lacy, my word is bond" Wolfe declared.

"I know you will baby, I know you will" I said rubbing his hand.

Wolfe's driver was at the airport to pick us up. It felt good to be back in familiar surroundings. I was exhausted and so was Wolfe. Shy Ann woke up with puffy eyes, she was quiet. I held her in the back of the truck with all the love I had. I stroked her curly hair from her face. Wolfe stared at both of us; I wanted to know his thoughts but didn't ask.

When we pulled up at Wolfe's house cars were around.

"Looks like you got company", I said as we got out of the car.

"Yeah the crew is here, we need each other right now", Wolfe stated.

I understood what he meant, when we walked in I was surprised to see Melissa was there with Sash, Karen and a beautiful woman sat beside her whom I assumed was her girlfriend-they sat hand and hand. A couple of more guys were there that looked familiar to me from the shops. Kem was there watching the news. Man-Man was next to Kem, Wolfe reintroduced me and ShyAnn to the ones I knew and introduced us to the ones I never met, Shy Ann ran up to Melissa and Melissa picked her up and hugged her tight. I hugged Melissa tighter; I missed my friend tears flowed down my eyes. I went and hugged everyone in the room giving my condolences for their loss, the ones I knew and didn't know.

Karen was much more welcoming to me today than last time we met. She hugged me tight, the type of hug that told me that I was okay with her. Everyone's heart was heavy but we were maintaining. I took Shy Ann up to a spare bedroom but was surprised when I cut the light on; the room was decorated similar to the one in the cabin. I was shocked. Shy Ann ran and started playing with all the toys that was in the room. Wolfe did this; he prepared this room for Shy Ann even when I told him that we were moving to the condo. I started to cry, this man was something else.

"This is my new room mama?" ShyAnn asked while pushing a plastic vacuum cleaner over her plush carpet.

"Umm yes, Wolfe made this especially for you", I stated.

"I like Wolfe mommy, he's always doing nice things for me", she said making me smile.

"I see you found my other surprise", Wolfe said standing at the door.

I hugged and kissed him deep, "You are everything to me", I said in sincerity.

"I love you baby girl", he stated and pecked my lips.

"Hey ShyAnn, check out this cool T.V." Wolfe stated and hit a button. Sponge bob popped on.

"Yay, Sponge bob", ShyAnn shouted with the biggest smile. I needed to see her smile like this.

"And this is all mines?" she asked with big eyes.

"Yes it's all yours, I will teach you how to use it later", Wolfe said with his arm around me.

ShyAnn ran up to Wolfe and hugged his leg, "Thanks Wolfe".

Wolfe bent down eye to eye with her, "I'm very sorry what happened to you tonight, but I am going to do whatever I can to take care of you and mommy okay?"

"I know you will", she said staring at him.

"Good", he said and gently squeezed her nose.

Melissa was watching at the door smiling, "Hey Mel come play with me, I am the doctor and you are the patient", ShyAnn announced holding out a plastic chart.

"Yes Ma'am, well doctor I am not feeling well today", Melissa dramatized for ShyAnn and sat on the carpet with her.

Wolfe and I went downstairs, music played low and everyone was talking amongst each other. Wolfe made me and him a drink; we sat on one of his couches facing everyone.

Karen asked Wolfe if she can speak with him in privacy, he got up. I looked at this man, his inner circle and thought how blessed he was. He had his life right here. He was the boss, well respected, loved, and humble and honored by many plus he loved me. I felt peace in my heart.

Kem came over to me, "You okay Brown Eyes?" He asked.

"I will be, and you how are you doing?" I asked concerned.

"Day by day is all I can say, day by day" Kem stated.

"I know that's right", I replied.

Karen and Wolfe entered the room and Karen asked for everyone's attention.

"Hey we appreciate everyone coming out tonight. We all here tonight is family. We are all dealing with this horrific death of our friend. All arrangements have been made for his memorial; we will lay him to rest honorably. The streets are talking, let them talk we lost family we don't owe the streets or the public anything. When yawl are in the shops keep any conversation about Pete to a minimum I mean we can't control people but you can maintain your quarters just asking for the respect of his death".

We continued to listen to Karen as she spoke strongly and was looking each of us in the eyes. A lot of what she was saying was powerful. Wolfe stood next to her with his hands clasp in front of him, looking at me from time to time. I would flash a smile at him that said it's going to be okay. Once Karen was done we sat around just talking, most of the other guys left and Karen and her girl, Sasha and Melissa, Kem and Wolfe and I sat around talking, and getting to know each other better.

Wolfe wanted everyone's attention "Listen, this week we are going to give Pete a good homecoming that's a promise, but this shit has been heavy on all of us. I don't want to get into detail right now, but I'm proposing that all of us in this room think about taking a needed vacation for like a week to clear our minds, wash some of this drama off of us-like a fresh start".

Karen stood up and raised her glass "I agree on that, we all family here now it'll give us a chance to get to know each other more and find some peace and relaxation", she looked at me and smiled.

Kem added, "I'm down for that for real, some blue water, sandy beaches, I'm all in" he raised his glass in the air,

Sash and Melissa agreed,

I looked at Melissa and smiled wide, she smiled back wider,

Everyone else raised their glasses and bottles in the air. I was smiling a much needed vacation I thought with a new family and the man I loved.

Melissa and Sash was the first to leave, then Kem and then Karen and her girlfriend. Once Wolfe and I were alone I went to check on Shy she fell asleep on the floor. I put her in her plush bed and came to Wolfe.

"We are going to stay here for a little while, we need too", I told Wolfe.

Wolfe hugged me tight, "I was hoping you said that Lace, I need you baby".

We kissed, "I need you too baby, and thank you for loving me".

He chuckled, "No, thank you for loving me".

We kissed passionately. Wolfe undressed me and himself we took a long hot shower together, we made love in the shower, then on the bed, then on the dresser and we ended on the floor next to the bed. Let's just say it was magical.

WOLFE

MEXICO

Three months passed

Time was flying by, Pete's home going was sad but we all did the very best that we could and it turned out well. The church was filled to capacity with people outside and lines around the corner. Karen did most of the arrangements and Lacy and I did our part. I was a blessed man to have these women in my life.

My mother and Mrs. Wilson did all the cooking, tables of food sat in my kitchen and dining room. I couldn't have done it without them. I never had so many people in my house before. But for Pete I didn't care it was all worth it. His aunt didn't want his urn and from his letter he wanted me to keep it. We picked a blue and silver urn that sat in my living room; Pete will always be with me.

Lacy moved into her condo after staying with me for a month after we cremated Pete. I appreciated her company; I needed my lady with me. I understand her wanting her independence. She stays with me at least three or four days a week. Sometime she brings Shy Ann with her. Shy Ann has met Mrs. Wilson's grandchildren which are her age so she has a posse of new friends when she comes over.

The vacation that we are planning is now in effect. Karen is making all the arrangements now. I have an investment account with over $200k I'm going to use some of that money to pay for all of us to go. Karen thought I was crazy and wanted to contribute her part, I told her she better bite her tongue. She has been my wonder woman since we were kids the least I can do is treat her to this. And everyone else has just been supportive and loving it's just something I want to do.

I situated Pete's belongings and money. The store sold, I gave his people their share and donated the rest to charity. I didn't want any of Pete's money, I had more than enough money and my money was building in many different accounts. My pops taught me how to manage my money and invest from a teenager. I used that knowledge on the streets and became successful in my businesses.

We decided to bring my mom and Mrs. Wilson along with us on vacation, they were excited and both loved ShyAnn, she would have two women standing in as grandmothers for her that love her. My mother was immediately drawn to her. She was waiting for me to have my own baby but fell in love with ShyAnn hands down.

I rented a private jet to hold all twelve of us; I ask Mrs. Wilson if she could bring her granddaughter Jasmine so that ShyAnn can have a playmate, she was more than happy to bring her. Our destination was Cancun Mexico. I had time share with a villa, Me and Lacy, Karen and her girlfriend, Sash and Melissa, Kem and his new flame stayed in that one. I rented a villa right next door for my mom and Mrs. Wilson and the girls.

Once the driver dropped us off we headed in and started unpacking.

LACY

Arriving in Cancun

Wolfe really went all out for this trip. The whole experience was exhilarating. I never saw ShyAnn so happy. Melissa and I shopped until we dropped. I used the 5000 credit card that Wolfe gave us to shop.

Most of our new clothes came from Melissa's boutique. She was hesitant at first but I talked her into it, she was the sister I never had and she has always had my back. I was honored to spoil us. She said that Wolfe was spoiling all of us and not even knowing it. It was true he was a giving man no doubt about it.

I was really tired on the jet; I slept most of the flight. My thoughts went to Bradley for a moment. He's been trying to reach out to me but I have nothing to say to him.

Wolfe and I was tested, both results came back negative for all STD's and HIV. That was a new life breathed into us. We are to be tested every year consistently to make sure. Wolfe and I no longer use condoms. I knew I was just as wrong as Bradley and I made up my mind that I would reach out to him sometime in the future I just wasn't ready to do it now.

Wolfe helped me find a nice size studio, I was super excited. Mikey came on full time and I hired an administrative assistant to do all booking and paperwork. I have a temp that comes in the days I'm not there to help Mikey on the shoots and developing. Everything was working out nicely.

I picked up the last things from the garage when Bradley wasn't there. I didn't want decorate too much at the condo because I was sure I would be moving in with Wolfe in six months. But I needed this adjustment period for ShyAnn. She asks for Bradley every now and then but she is hands down attached to Wolfe. I kept in the back of my mind that if this somehow does not work with Wolfe that I will not date anyone exclusively for a long time. I wasn't going to pass men in and out of her life. But Wolfe is a keeper.

Once we arrived at the villa I kissed Shy and off she went with Ms. Wilson, Ms. Harris and Jasmine. The girls wanted to get in the pool they were excited, laughing and giggling the whole way. The villa was amazing it had six bedrooms, Wolfe and I had the exclusive master suite, it reminded of the cabin. I took pictures of the inside. I made all of us take pictures, we made crazy faces, Melissa took a picture of Wolfe and I that I knew I was going to enlarge and hang in my condo and his house. It was something about that picture that mended us together perfectly. I couldn't stop looking at it.

WOLFE

Surprises

On our third day in I had Karen organize a group dinner on the beach. We hired a service to do all the cooking and serving. The table was one long rectangle decorated with a white table cloth, white lit candles going down the table, with wine and liquor bottles in silver buckets of ice. Three plates sat at each chair with fancy spoons, folks, and knives, it was beautiful. We picked out all our favorite foods to have it prepared and served. The liquor was flowing, bottles sat on the table on ice. The cool night air felt good. The ocean was splashing waves, it was a beautiful scene. Lacy had her camera she was taking pictures of everything.

"Baby girl, come sit down and relax. I want you to enjoy your meal", I said.

Lacy came and kissed me, "Just a couple of more of your mom and Ms. Wilson and I'm done-promise", she said smiling.

Lacy was so beautiful the sun gave her a beautiful tan that ignited her brown eyes and a beautiful glow. I was in love with this woman. Once she sat down I stood up and ask for everyone's attention. Once I got it I said, "I have a few things I just want to say before we all enjoy this delicious meal being prepared for us, first of all we all have had an hell of year one way or another, problems came in each of our lives but because we had each other we made it through. Life is about love and goodness, each of us demonstrates that one way or another.

" If you would have told me that I would be standing here without my best friend today yet with the woman I love last year I would have thought you was crazy. We carried each other through some rough times.

" To my mom who has been there for me, I want you to know that I love you very much, to my brother Kem, new beginning brother, to Karen who has been my sister from childhood you are an amazing woman.

"Sash brother you know what it is we for life, Melissa welcome and thank you for always being there for the woman I love. And Ms. Wilson you are like a second mom to me thanks for all you do for all of us. And last but never least."

I looked at Lacy and extended my hand for her to come to me. I took the box out of my pocket Karen sent ShyAnn up to stand next to me. Lacy's eyes widened and tears started to build up.

"To the woman that I love with all I have, in front of the people we love, tonight I am asking for you to be my wife- Lacy Grant will you marry me?"

The tears didn't stop flowing from her eyes. ShyAnn was hugging her leg. She lifted her head and looked at the sky as if it had the answers for her.

"Yes, without any doubt I will marry you Mr. Harris", she said.

I put the two carat diamond cut ring on her finger and kissed her hand. I reached down and picked up Shy Ann, and kissed my soon to be wife.

Everyone stood up and clapped, my mother and Melissa came to us first then everyone else followed. I planned on doing this from the night in the living room when I proposed it. Karen was the only one that knew. She was on board, she grew to love

Lacy when she seen her true loyalty and love to me. Karen helped me pick the ring out.

We all stood around, the waiters watched and clapped in amazement. Champagne went around the table. When all was done and we was going to sit down, Lacy asked for everyone's attention as she wiped the tears from her eyes.

"I just want to thank everyone here, a new family and a new beginning for ShyAnn and me. I couldn't ask God for anything better at least I thought, then God blew me away again, I was going to wait for this but this is the perfect time. Wolfe, you have given me so much since we met, you have showed me unconditional love, support and protection and strength. Besides my father you are the most gentle, most humble man I have run across in my life. I always told you that I wanted to do something for you and you would tell me that, that wasn't necessary but tonight baby I want to share with our family".

She walked up to me and took my hand and placed it on her stomach, "You're going to be a daddy Mr. Harris", she said smiling.

My mother screamed in happiness, I was shocked. I rubbed her stomach in amazement, "Baby girl", I said hugging and kissing her.

I looked her in her eyes I didn't see anyone else but Lacy "Yo, I can't believe this baby", our hug brought me to tears. I didn't want to let her go, she was carrying my seed.

Everyone at the table started chanting, and giving us love pumping their fist in the air. I couldn't believe how my life was turning out but I was so happy and blessed.

After dinner was over, the waiters were cleaning up everything Lacy and I sat on the beach on a white blanket, looking at the ocean. Lacy laid against my chest, the waves was splashing lightly, the stars was bright in the sky, I was going to be a daddy I rubbed her stomach, her ring sparkled. Life has a way of hurting us and loving us all at the same time. I finally have all the things I ever wanted. I was a blessed man!

Almost the end

Dear God,

It's been a year since Wolfe asked me to marry him, our son Christian Peter Harris was born on May 9, 2014 he was born 8lbs 6 0z. Thank you for giving us a beautiful healthy baby boy. He is just as handsome as his dad and grandfathers. We named him Christian after Wolfe's dad, and Peter of course after Wolfe's best friend. He is a true blessing. ShyAnn loves him so much and she shows so much protection over him. I smile every time I see it. When Wolfe looks at his son, it's no greater feeling in the world, and loves ShyAnn just as much.

We moved in with Wolfe once we returned from Mexico, it just felt good to do. I sub leased my condo to Mikey, he was happy to take it he was looking for a place and it just made sense to do. My studio is doing very well, I don't take as much pictures as I did before but Mikey has it under control. We have new marketing tactics to get more clients; it rocketed into hiring two temp photographers.

Melissa and Sash are exclusive and he really loves her. It's amazing the ones you think aren't ready for commitments are. Melissa is firm that she's taking it slow, but like Wolfe Sash spoils her and she loves it. I am so happy for them. They are baby Christians God Parents. After what happen to Pete, everyone has calmed down from the club scene even Kem has a steady girlfriend.

Wolfe is in the process of opening Laundromats, he said he's been thinking about it for awhile but now that Christian has been born he wants to leave a legacy to Shyann and him. Shyann loves Wolfe, by the end of the year Wolfe wants to adopt Shyann legally. I'm so happy; he was serious when he said he was going to take care of us.

Ms. Harris and Ms. Wilson help us out so much with babysitting. Since the baby has been born we have

Sunday dinners every weekend here at the house after church. I started working out again trying to lose the last 10 lbs of my baby weight.

I finally spoke to Bradley. It took me months but once we got together the ill feelings died. He comes by from time to time to visit, he misses ShyAnn a lot and she misses him.

Bradley explained how hard it was to be a bisexual man. His family still isn't speaking with him especially his father, his mother will take his calls but he cannot visit, and he has a good relationship with his sister. I felt sorry for Bradley once he told me his story from beginning to end. Bradley explained that he was sexually abused when he was a child by an older male cousin from his dad's side of the family. When he finally had the guts to tell his father, his father went into a rage denying that could ever happen. It confused Bradley from childhood, but as he got older he said he desired men more than women. I'm just glad that I didn't get any disease or vice versa.

Lord, I understand that everything in this world happens for a reason. Sometimes we really never understand why certain situations are allowed or certain people come across our path we must just pay attention. I have never been as happy as I am right now. I have the man that I love two beautiful healthy children, a strong home base a booming business and new and great people in my life.

Wolfe and I talk so much about our lives; we know that his father and my parents are guiding our lives with your grace from Heaven. Our Wedding date is February 15th; we are going to have a small wedding and a big honeymoon.

I ask for you to forgive me for all my sins, and thank you for all my blessings.

None of us ask to come here, life is a gift- we have our highs and we have our lows. We are going to mess up a lot and do things we aren't suppose to. The seeds we plant are the harvest we reap. Although it's been a tough year, it's been a year of blessing. I thank you with all the love I have within me.

Lacy

The End